Stephanie

TONIGHT AND FOREVER

"This is a terrific book, filled with love in all its guises. Ms. Jackson brings passion and tenderness, faith and trust, together with friendship and does it so well."

—*The Paperback Forum*

"*Tonight and Forever*. . . is so well written and entertaining that readers of all genres will enjoy the experience."

—*Affaire de Coeur*

"Mrs. Jackson's impressive debut novel is a silk and satin fantasy grounded in sensual reality."

—*Romantic Times BOOKreviews*

"*Tonight and Forever* is a genuine love story. . . an outstanding experience readers won't forget for a long time."

—*Rendezvous*

Laughter cannot mask a heavy heart. When the laughter ends, the grief remains.

—*Proverbs* 14:13

BRENDA JACKSON

TONIGHT AND FOREVER

TONIGHT AND FOREVER

An Arabesque novel published by Kimani Press December 2007

First published by Kensington Publishing Corp. in 1995.

ISBN-13: 978-1-61523-650-3

Printed in U.S.A.

THE MADARIS FAMILY AND FRIENDS SERIES

Dear Readers,

I love writing family sagas, and I am so happy that Harlequin is reissuing my very first family series, the Madaris family. It's been twelve years and fifty books since I first introduced the Madaris family. During that time, this special family and their friends have warmed their way into readers' hearts. I am ecstatic about sharing these award-winning stories with readers all over again—especially those who have never met the Madaris clan up close and personal—in this special-edition reissue, with more to follow in the coming months.

I never dreamed when I penned my first novel, *Tonight and Forever,* and introduced the Madaris family, that what I was doing was taking readers on a journey where heartfelt romance, sizzling passion and true love awaited them at every turn. I had no idea that the Madaris family and their friends would become characters that readers would come to know and care so much about. I invite you to relax, unwind and see what all the hoopla is about. Let Justin, Dex, Clayton, Uncle Jake and their many friends indulge your fantasies with love stories that are so passionate and sizzling they will take your breath away. There is nothing better than falling in love with one of those Madaris men and their circle of friends and family.

For a complete listing of all the books in this series, as well as the reissue publication dates for each novel, please visit my Web site at www.brendajackson.net.

If you would like to receive my monthly newsletter please visit and sign up at http://www.brendajackson.net/page/newsletter.htm.

I also invite you to drop me an e-mail at WriterBJackson@aol.com. I love hearing from my readers.

All the best,

Brenda Jackson

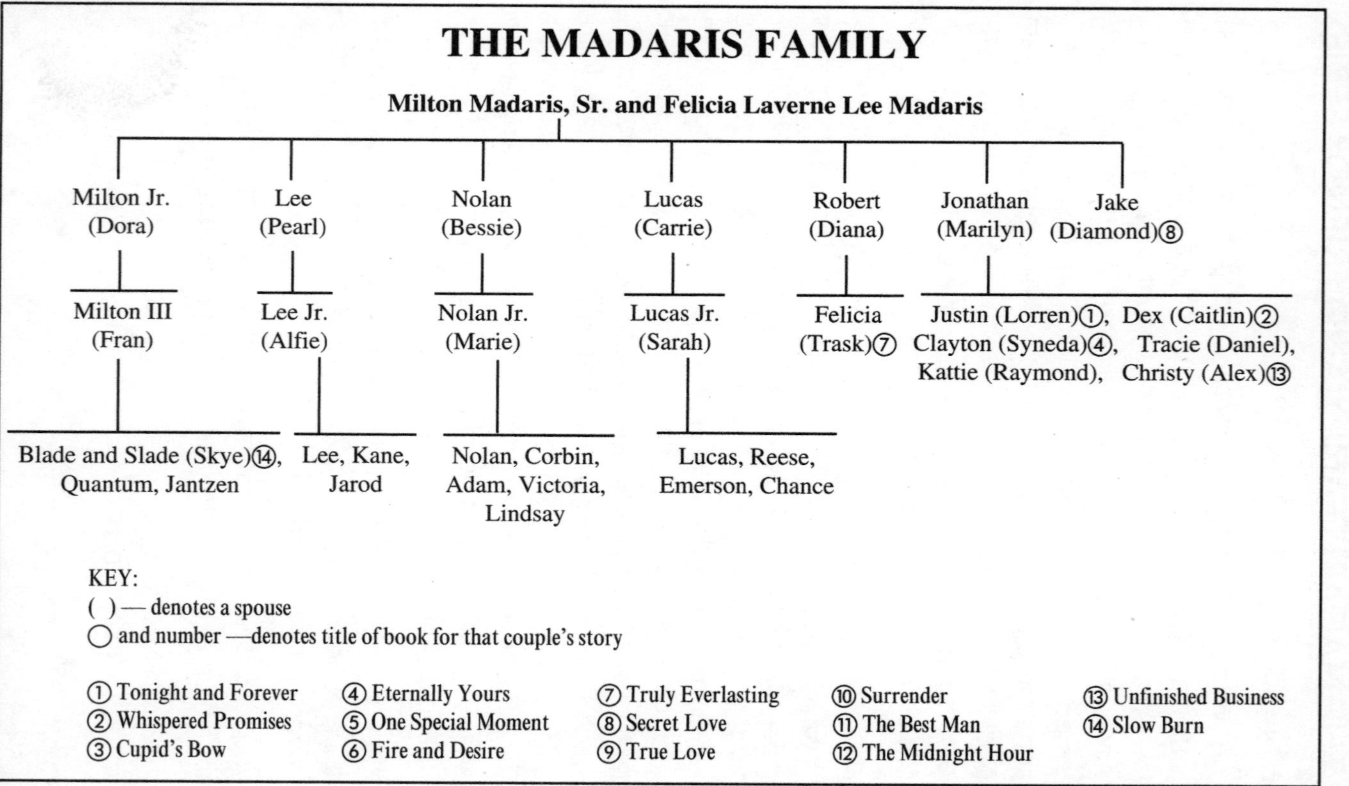

THE MADARIS FAMILY
Milton Madaris, Sr. and Felicia Laverne Lee Madaris
Milton Jr. (Dora)
Lee (Pearl)
Nolan (Bessie)
Lucas (Carrie)
Robert (Diana)
Jonathan (Marilyn)
Jake (Diamond)⑧
Milton III (Fran)
Lee Jr. (Alfie)
Nolan Jr. (Marie)
Lucas Jr. (Sarah)
Felicia (Trask)⑦
Justin (Lorren)①, Dex (Caitlin)②
Clayton (Syneda)④, Tracie (Daniel),
Kattie (Raymond), Christy (Alex)⑬
Blade and Slade (Skye)⑭, Quantum, Jantzen
Lee, Kane, Jarod
Nolan, Corbin, Adam, Victoria, Lindsay
Lucas, Reese, Emerson, Chance
KEY:
( ) — denotes a spouse
◯ and number —denotes title of book for that couple's story
① Tonight and Forever
② Whispered Promises
③ Cupid's Bow
④ Eternally Yours
⑤ One Special Moment
⑥ Fire and Desire
⑦ Truly Everlasting
⑧ Secret Love
⑨ True Love
⑩ Surrender
⑪ The Best Man
⑫ The Midnight Hour
⑬ Unfinished Business
⑭ Slow Burn

THE MADARIS FRIENDS

Maurice and Stella Grant
|
Trevor (Corinthians)⑥, Regina (Mitch)⑪

Angelique Hamilton Chenault
|
Sterling Hamilton (Colby)⑤, Nicholas Chenault (Shayla)⑨

Kyle Garwood (Kimara)③

Ashton Sinclair (Netherland)⑩

Drake Warren (Tori)⑫

Trent Jordache (Brenna)⑨

Nedwyn Lansing (Diana)⑭

KEY:
( ) — denotes a spouse
◯ and number —denotes title of book for that couple's story

① Tonight and Forever
② Whispered Promises
③ Cupid's Bow
④ Eternally Yours
⑤ One Special Moment
⑥ Fire and Desire
⑦ Truly Everlasting
⑧ Secret Love
⑨ True Love
⑩ Surrender
⑪ The Best Man
⑫ The Midnight Hour
⑬ Unfinished Business
⑭ Slow Burn

Acknowledgment

I would like to give a heartfelt thank-you to the following people:

To the man who has been my husband, best friend, love of my life and the wind beneath my wings for thirty-five years, Gerald Jackson, Sr.

To my two sons, Gerald, Jr. and Brandon, who are proud of their mom, the writer.

To a group of special friends who were kind enough to let me borrow their time—Denise Coleman, Pat Sams, Agnes Dixon, Betty Hodge, Juanita Heard, Sandra Nottenkamper, Lynn Sims, Marsher Boyd, Delores Young, Sunnie Dodd, Cynthia Grissett, Pat Render and Emma Upshaw.

To the members of the First Coast Romance Writers for their constant encouragement; to Debbie, Anita and Marge for their constant readings and invaluable feedback of the book in progress.

To Vivian Stephens for her timely words of encouragement.

To Syneda Walker, a very special friend.

To all my family, friends and coworkers for their undying support.

To my eighth-grade classmates at Northwestern Junior High School, Jacksonville, Florida, who enjoyed my stories even back then.

Last but definitely not least, I thank God for being the giver of all good and perfect gifts and from whom all blessings flow.

Chapter 1

"She's absolutely breathtaking."

The words emerged as a mere whisper from Justin Madaris's lips before he realized he'd spoken his thoughts aloud. Preferring at the moment to be apart from the growing crowd, he stood tall, a solitary figure, barely distinguishable in the shadows, as his mesmerized gaze followed the woman circulating among the other party guests. A seductive gracefulness marked her every movement. Glossy dark brown hair, stylishly cut, cascaded over her shoulders, accentuating her perfect features and complementing her nutmeg skin. She was, simply put, a strikingly beautiful woman.

Justin absently loosened the knot in his tie as a

thrumming heat pulsed deep within him. The woman had a stimulating effect on his vital signs.

Who is she? he wondered, lifting a glass to his lips. The sparkling taste of the vintage wine was blotted from his mind as he continued to engage in a visual exploration of her body. The backless black dress was stunning. The delicate fabric clung subtly, defining her shapely figure. He couldn't help noticing that the side slit of the outfit revealed one long beautiful leg. He'd bet her legs fit perfectly around a man's waist while they made love.

Instinctively he took a step forward, intent on finding out who she was. His face dimpled into a smile. The woman had thoroughly aroused his curiosity and totally captured his interest.

There's nothing like seeing old friends again, Lorren Jacobs thought, making her way through the room filled with numerous people from her past. Like her, most of them had spent their childhoods here at what used to be a foster home run by Paul and Nora Phillips. To them, this large house located in the small town of Ennis, Texas—a skip and a hop from Dallas—was home.

Tonight they'd returned and had gone all out to host the party honoring Mama Nora's sixty-fifth birthday. Nora and her husband, Paul, who'd died six years ago, had been instrumental in shaping their lives, providing them with food and shelter, love, friendship, and guidance.

A smile touched Lorren's lips as she glanced around the room. She knew that no expense had been spared. The food committee had special caterers flown in from New York. The decorating committee had depleted every florist shop for miles. The entertainment committee had hired a popular disc jockey to alternate with a well-known jazz band from New Orleans. A small army of people had turned out to celebrate the birthday of a woman who was a pillar of the community, a supporter of noble causes, and a dear friend.

Lorren stopped to hold a brief conversation with Mr. Monroe, the principal of her old high school, when she suddenly had the strangest feeling she was being watched. Scanning the room, she could find no reason for the peculiar sensation.

When her conversation with Mr. Monroe ended, she made her way to the buffet table, passing out quick smiles of recognition and several words of greeting to those she met. The massive spread of food looked delectable. But before she could pick up a plate, someone called her name.

Turning in the direction of the familiar voice, she came face-to-face with her closest friend, Syneda Walters, who had also grown up in the Phillipses' household. Long luxurious golden bronze curls tumbled over Syneda's shoulders, softly framing an attractive light brown face. Syneda's eyes, sea green in color, were perfect for the long curling sweep of lashes veiling them.

"So far, so good. The caterers outdid themselves. Everything's perfect," Syneda said excitedly.

Lorren smiled. "That's the reason we made you head of the food committee, Syneda. You could be counted on to make everything first-class. We didn't give you the nickname 'Classy Sassy' all those years ago for nothing."

Both women laughed. Their sound mingled with the joviality of the other guests in the room. "Let's go in here," Syneda said, pulling Lorren through a pair of double doors at the far end of the room. "It's escape time," she teased. They stepped into a large, book-lined study and closed the door behind them.

"I meant to tell you earlier how sharp your hair looks. That style looks super on you," Syneda said. "I never understood why you began wearing your hair short."

Lorren managed a half smile. "Scott preferred it that way." Saying her ex-husband's name evoked memories of a hellish marriage and the very real relief of her divorce.

"Hey, as far as this sister is concerned, there's a number of things Scott Howard preferred," Syneda responded tersely, not trying to hide the contempt she felt for the man. "One of which was being a fool and not appreciating what he had."

You better shut her up, Lorren's inner voice warned, *or homegirl will begin sounding off on Scott's cruddy attributes from now till kingdom come. Even though you agree with all of them, he's the last person you want to think about tonight,* she thought, studying the woman standing before her.

The two of them were bonded by a strong friendship. Syneda had been maid of honor at Lorren's wedding, then two years later had helped her through a shattering divorce. Although they were close, they were completely opposite in personality and temperament. Lorren had majored in English literature in college while Syneda had ventured into law and now worked for one of the most prestigious law firms in New York.

Lorren also knew her best friend had achieved the life she'd always wanted. Syneda had been adamant about not getting seriously involved with anyone until she'd blossomed in her career.

Lorren's own life hadn't turned out quite the way she had planned. Unlike Syneda, she had always hoped to be happily married by her twenty-sixth birthday, with at least one child—possibly another on the way—have a beautiful beach house on the Pacific coast where she'd be typing out her second or third award-winning book. With her birthday a few months away, all her dreams seemed unattainable.

"So much for a breather," Loren said, pulling Syneda toward the door. She didn't want to dwell on her lost dreams any longer. "Let's go back."

"Okay," Syneda agreed, sensing Lorren's melancholic mood. "The night's still a baby, and if we're lucky, we'll run into a couple of fine, unattached brothers here."

"Maybe," Lorren answered uninterestedly. "I've noticed you're not lacking attention tonight."

Syneda raised an arched brow at what could have been taken as a dig. "You wouldn't either if you'd loosen up, girlfriend, and stop being so uptight around men. Don't think I haven't been checking you out. And if I've picked up on it, so will Mama Nora, *if* she hasn't already. The last thing we need is for her to start worrying about any of us. She's done enough of that over the years."

Lorren released a smothered sigh. She'd hoped her self-imposed barriers of protection hadn't been obvious. "You're right." As they left the study she asked, "Are you still flying out first thing in the morning?"

"Yeah. I need to finalize an important case, but I'll be back Monday night. Then I'll be here for at least a week."

Lorren smiled. "Great. I can't wait to have lunch at Sophie's Diner."

Syneda grinned. "Neither can I. I hear their onion burger hasn't changed. You still get more onions than burger."

Laughter erupted between the two women again.

"The woman in the black dress, do you know her?" Justin asked the tall, distinguished-looking older man who happened to be the brother of the honoree.

Senator Roman Malone's gaze followed Justin's, and a thoughtful smile curved his mouth. "That's Lorren Jacobs. She lived here with Nora and Paul, then moved away when she graduated from high school about seven years ago."

"Married?"

"Not anymore."

"Widowed? Divorced?"

"She's divorced."

"Where's she living now?"

"Was in California, but Nora mentioned earlier tonight Lorren's moved back to Ennis." The senator grinned. "Son, you ask more questions than the *National Enquirer,* and I've given all the information I intend to." His smile faded. "But I'll give you fair warning, Justin. Nora also mentioned that Lorren's divorce left her with deep scars."

Justin glanced across the room at the woman dressed in black. His gaze took in everything about her. He suddenly remembered things he'd noticed earlier that hadn't made sense.

Now they did.

She seemed to avoid one-on-one conversation. She seemed more comfortable in a group. And so far, she'd turned down every man who'd asked her to dance.

The senator peered up at him. "I can tell by the gleam in your eyes, you aren't taking me seriously."

Justin's face split into a wide grin. "As an old college pal of Dad's, you should know a Madaris can't resist a challenge."

The senator laughed. "Do you want an introduction?"

"No, not yet. I want to enjoy the view some more," Justin replied before walking away.

* * *

Lorren, absorbed in the conversation swirling around her between Syneda and Senator Malone, who'd come to join them, again experienced an eerie feeling of being watched. Another quick scan of the room revealed nothing, but the feeling persisted. A few minutes later she took still another glance around the room.

Then she saw him.

He stood alone, casually leaning against the wall. His stance was formidable, and his gaze scanned her assessingly. The look he was giving her came from a man who knew what he liked and had no qualms about showing it.

Lorren's pulse skittered when his gaze moved appreciatively from her face and downward, over the curves of her figure and legs before returning to her face again. She quickly turned her back to him but, unable to resist a glance, discovered his gaze still glued to her, and, to make matters worse, he was heading her way. Watching him advance with long, purposeful strides, she couldn't tear her gaze from his.

Dressed in an expensive suit tailored to fit his lithe, hard body like a glove, his aura of rugged masculinity suggested he'd be just as relaxed in a pair of well-worn jeans and a chambray shirt. He appeared to be well over six feet tall, and the muscles rippling beneath the suit jacket told her his athletic build came as a result of vigorous physical activity.

His face was arrestingly carved in sharp angles and fine lines. Close-cropped, curly black hair, and a neatly trimmed mustache accentuated his sensual upper lip and emphasized the mystery in eyes the color of chocolate chips. The healthy glow of his chestnut skin tempted her to touch it to see if it really felt like warm satin.

Lorren blinked. She suspected she was finally losing her sanity. Two years of pain and humiliation had somehow slipped her mind, and she'd become utterly fascinated by a total stranger. She had to hand it to the man for giving special meaning to the description tall, dark, and handsome.

"Good evening."

"Dr. Madaris. Come join us," Senator Malone said. "Do you know everyone?" he asked, indicating the others.

"No, I don't, Senator," Justin answered smoothly, scanning the group. He quickly returned his gaze to Lorren and focused on her features. Up close she was even more beautiful. She possessed eyes the color of rich caramel, a straight nose, a nicely rounded chin, and a beautifully shaped mouth.

"Well, then," the senator replied. "Syneda Walters, Lorren Jacobs, meet Dr. Justin Madaris."

Lorren's heart hammered against her ribs from the contact of Justin's hand in a brief handshake. Long fingers gently squeezed hers before releasing them. He elicited the most powerful and intense physical reaction she'd ever experienced. It totally unnerved her. His eyes glowed with intense male interest under thick black lashes. A shiver of warning passed through her.

"Lorren, would you like to dance?" Justin asked.

His voice, deep and sensual, stirred something elemental in her blood. Refusal hovered on her lips, but when she caught Syneda's gaze, the message clearly said, *Girl, don't be a fool. Go for it!*

Against her better judgment, she said, "Yes."

The DJ had put on a slow number by Luther Vandross when Justin took Lorren's arm and led her toward the dance floor. She could feel the gentle imprint of his fingers on her skin and shivered.

"You're trembling. Are you cold?" he asked. His voice, low, strong, yet seductive, caressed the words he'd spoken. His gaze left hers and dropped to her arms as if checking for goose bumps. He returned his attention to her.

"No," she replied coolly, not liking the effect he had on her. She was unprepared for the sheer power of his masculinity. He had a magnetic, compelling charm that undoubtedly paved his way into a lot of women's hearts, not to mention their beds, she thought. When he pulled her into his arms, she tipped her head to study him.

"You hesitated before accepting my invitation to dance. Somebody tell you I've got two left feet?"

Caught off guard by his teasing, Lorren fumbled for an answer.

"No. But you didn't expect me to rush into your arms, did you?" she replied, forcing a demure smile.

"I wouldn't have complained if you had," he replied, his slow smile taunting her.

Lorren raised her eyes to meet his. Big mistake. Looking into his eyes made her breasts tingle against the fabric of her dress.

"Nice perfume," he said. "What is it?"

"Beautiful," she replied in a controlled voice.

"How appropriate," Justin said silkily. His gaze settled on her full, inviting lips, glazed with a delicious shade of red that reminded him of strawberries. They were his favorite fruit.

Their eyes met. And that sharp awareness that had cut through Justin's body like an electric shock when they'd been introduced was there again. Although he was holding her close, it wasn't close enough. The small space separating their bodies teased his senses. He felt a definite attraction to this woman. She was one of the few women he'd met who could ignite rampant emotions within him. Her beautiful eyes reflected strong will and intelligence. Looking deeper, he saw hints of loneliness and pain in them that seemed to be an innate part of her.

Justin's compliment made Lorren's heart pound out an erratic rhythm. "Thanks." She'd noticed his gaze had shifted to her mouth. Her throat went dry. Suddenly feeling a little light-headed, she blamed it on the wine she'd had earlier, but knew better. *The last thing you need is another man messing with your mind. Mama Nora didn't raise a fool. You have enough sense to see this guy is walking, breathing trouble. You can bet your Gucci he's the type who goes after what he wants and won't stop until he gets it.* Her pulse quickened at the thought.

His closeness was drugging her senses, lulling her into a euphoria. But she had no intention of experiencing a sexual high off him. She decided that holding a polite conversation would be the best way to keep from responding to his magnetic charm. "So you're a doctor?"

"Yes, I am."

"Where?"

"Here in Ennis. I took over Dr. Powers's practice when he retired ten months ago."

"Oh, I didn't know." Dr. Powers had been a very well liked and respected general physician in Ennis for as long as Lorren could remember. "I'm surprised the people accepted you as his replacement."

Justin's laugh sounded low and sexy. "Why?"

"You certainly don't look like a doctor."

"Oh? How's a doctor supposed to look?"

Lorren stared up at him as a flush stole into her cheeks. *Not like he should grace the covers of a magazine,* she thought.

"What I mean is, a lot of people in this town are set in their ways. They think competency comes with age, and compared to Doc Powers, you're rather young," she replied, proud of her quick thinking. There was no way she would tell him what she actually thought.

A sensuous smile came to life on his lips. "I don't consider thirty-five as being young. And I had no trouble being accepted in this town, once they saw my qualifications."

"You must be pretty good at what you do."

Justin grinned, his teeth strikingly white against his rich dark skin. "Yeah. I think so, and I haven't received any complaints so far," he murmured huskily.

Lorren drew a tremulous breath. They'd been talking about his profession, hadn't they? He had not even hinted at anything otherwise, but for some reason she felt he was saying more. "Where're you from?"

"Originally, I'm from Houston." He chuckled. "So I better not hear anything raunchy about the Texans. I still have a hard time accepting that this is Dallas Cowboys country. What a waste of spirit."

For the first time Lorren gave him a dazzling smile, one Justin felt was genuine. He doubted she had any idea just how beautiful she looked with that smile. The transformation was stunning. If he'd thought her attractive before, she was now devastatingly so. Her hair tumbled around her shoulders, framing her face and highlighting her features.

"I'll try remembering that during football season when the Cowboys kick the Texans' butts, big-time, Dr. Madaris."

Justin laughed. "Whoa! The lady gets kind of rowdy in defense of her favorite team. But I can handle that. No one was a bigger Cowboys fan than my wife. Whenever they lost to the Oilers, she took it personally, and somehow I paid dearly."

Lorren blinked twice. She didn't recall seeing a ring on his finger. "You're married?"

"Not anymore," he replied somberly. "My wife died ten years ago."

The deep emotion in his voice got Lorren's full attention. "I'm sorry."

"Me, too. Denise was a very special woman. She taught me a lot during the time we were together. She especially taught me never to take anyone or anything for granted. Life's too short. She was a very courageous woman. Even at the end, she had more guts than a lot of people I know."

"She died ten years ago? She had to be rather young," Lorren said.

Justin nodded. "Yes. She was twenty-four when she died of an inoperable brain tumor," he replied. "We were married only five years, but they were the greatest years of my life. We were both young, and I was struggling through med school, but we had something a lot of young couples don't have when they get married."

A lump formed in Lorren's throat. She moistened her lips. "What?"

"We had a firm belief in commitment and in the value of marriage. We took the minister's words to heart…to love and to honor, in sickness and in health, forsaking all others, till death do us part."

Lorren's eyes became misty. He'd lost a lot more

than she had, and apparently still believed in love. She couldn't help but think of Scott.

It was love at first sight, or so she'd thought at the time. During the months they'd dated, he'd been her knight in shining armor. But his sterling coating began tarnishing not long after their marriage. To be more precise, their problems began on their wedding night. Terrible regrets assailed her, and she looked into Justin's eyes.

Some unexplainable need pushed her to ask the next question. "Do you think you'll ever marry again, Justin?"

"Yes. Under the right circumstances, marriage is a pleasant and worthwhile institution. I believe in both love and marriage. It was meant for a man and woman to live together in holy matrimony."

Lorren frowned. "If you really believe that, then why haven't you remarried?"

He smiled. "So far, a woman hasn't come along who I can't imagine living my life without. Until she does, I'm going to remain single. I happen to believe in fate. If there's a woman out there, and we're destined to be together, I won't have to look for her. Fate will bring her to me."

Lorren gave his words some thought. She considered herself an intelligent woman who believed in reality. As far as she was concerned, his belief in fate was romantic and idealistic hogwash. Nothing in life was left to fate.

"I hate to sound cynical, but I don't share your

fairy-tale ideals on love and marriage. I stopped believing in both long ago. My ex-husband made absolutely sure of that."

Justin's throat tightened with the compelling look of pain in her eyes. For some reason that he couldn't explain, he wanted to pull her closer, surround her with his strength, and somehow remove the hurt shadowing her eyes.

"Whoever he was, Lorren, you're better off without him. Any man who makes a woman lose faith in love and marriage isn't fit to be called a husband, and doesn't deserve her devotion. And I hope he pays dearly for making you feel that way."

Lorren looked up at him. His eyes had darkened, his voice, although hard, had lowered slightly. The quiet solidity in his words touched her. His arms surrounded her, drawing her a little closer to his body. Her hands rested on his powerful shoulders, and she could feel his strength.

Reluctantly, he released her when the music came to an end. She felt an odd sense of loss.

"Thanks for the dance, Lorren." Justin led her from the dance floor to the bar set up on the other side of the room. "I understand you've moved back to Ennis."

Lorren couldn't help but smile at the thought of how fast news could travel in a small town. "Yes, that's right." The pressure of his hand on her back was light, but she could feel his long, masculine fingers. They seemed to burn hot, branding her sensitized skin.

"Will you join me for dinner tomorrow night?"

Lorren stared up at him. Getting through a dance with Justin had been tough enough. An entire evening in his presence was not in her game plan. Not now, not ever. "No, I'm sorry."

A probing query came into his eyes. "How about the following night?"

She smiled inwardly, doubting many women turned him down for anything. "I don't go out with strangers."

He chuckled. "We're no longer strangers, are we? However, if you want character references, I believe I can drum up a few."

"I'm sure you can, but I'll be busy."

"What about—"

"I'll be busy for quite some time, Justin," she cut in.

"How about a rain check?"

"Sorry, I don't give them. If you'll excuse me, I need to talk with Syneda about something." She walked off, feeling the heat of Justin's intense gaze on her back.

"Back so soon? I thought the two of you made a striking couple."

Lorren gave Syneda a piqued glare. "Girl, *pleaz*. Don't even think it."

A smile touched Syneda's lips. "Evidently Justin does, sister-girl. He's on his way back over here."

Lorren's heart skipped a beat. "He's probably going to ask you to dance this time."

Syneda gave her a pointed look. "I *don't* think so. It's obvious the brother is interested in you. He's *your* Dr. Madaris."

"He's not *my* anything. The man belongs to any woman who wants him."

Syneda laughed. "From the looks the two of you got while dancing, I would say there's quite a few."

When Justin was a few feet from them, Lorren whispered, "I'm going upstairs to the ladies' room. He's all yours. I'm sure you can handle him." She gave Syneda a huge smile before turning to walk off.

Lorren strode across the room and up the stairs. Upon reaching the top landing, she glanced around, remembering the newspapers, magazines, and schoolbooks that used to lie scattered around when she'd lived here. Now everything was neat and tidy. Even with the noise of the guests from below, she was acutely aware of the house's stillness compared to how it had been years ago when ten foster children had scampered through it.

The oversize house that had once been her home since the age of eight was now a rooming house. Mama Nora's boarders were college students who thought the forty-five-minute drive into Dallas was nothing compared to Mama Nora's down-home cooking, friendship, and grandmotherly disposition.

Leaning against the wall for a moment, Lorren suppressed a sigh. Syneda thought Justin was interested in her. Even if he was, once he discovered the truth about her, he'd realize pursuing her was a waste of time. Scott had made her painfully aware she was a woman incapable of fulfilling a man's needs and desires in the bedroom. Her sexual inadequacies, he'd claimed, were the reason he had sought out other women. He'd once described her as a prettily wrapped package he'd anxiously waited for, but once he'd unwrapped it, he'd been disappointed.

Lorren struggled to fight back tears that burned her eyes. She would never place herself in a position to have to deal with that type of disappointment and rejection from any man again. And if that meant shielding herself from the male world, and choosing a life of celibacy, then so be it. Somehow, she would continue to battle the pangs of loneliness that would often hit her.

Her thoughts shifted to Justin Madaris. He wasn't the only one who had been committed to wedding vows. In the beginning, so had she. She had stayed married to Scott for those two years, deeply believing in the minister's words that... What God has joined together...

But by the time their marriage had ended, she was only thankful to God for giving her the sense to accept she'd made a big mistake in her choice of a mate, and the courage to leave Scott when she had. No one, not even Syneda, knew completely what had finally driven her away from Scott. Even thinking about it made her feel ashamed.

Shaking off the despairing memories, she

returned downstairs and headed toward the table that held the huge punch bowl.

"Baby, are you enjoying yourself?"

Lorren turned toward the voice. The aged face of the older woman couldn't shroud evidence of past years of radiant beauty. Her hair, completely gray, was pulled back and up in a twisted bun.

Lorren smile. "Yes, Mama Nora. I am."

"You all did me well tonight. I feel so blessed."

"We're the ones who are blessed for being recipients of Papa Paul's and your unselfish love. Not only did you open your home to us, but you opened your hearts as well."

"Paul and I couldn't have kids of our own. That saddened us. We'd always wanted a big family. In the end, we got just what we wanted."

Lorren chuckled. "Bet you got more than you bargained for."

Nora Phillips reached out and embraced Lorren. "We never thought so. And I'm glad you came back home, baby."

"Me, too."

"Good evening, Ms. Nora. Lorren."

The deep familiar masculine voice made Lorren turn around.

"Dr. Madaris, I'm glad to see that you and Lorren have met already." Nora's sparkling eyes darted between the couple.

A disarming grin covered Justin's face. "Yes, ma'am, we met earlier tonight."

"Good. Did Lorren tell you she's a writer?"

Justin gave Lorren a smile that sent her pulse racing. "No, ma'am, she didn't mention it. What type of books do you write, Lorren?"

"Children's stories," Lorren replied, eyeing Mama Nora and Justin. It was obvious Mama Nora liked him.

"Children's stories? That's interesting," Justin said.

His comment drew Lorren's gaze to his mesmerizing eyes. As her heart skipped a beat, she became aware of a heat curling deep within her.

The disc jockey began playing an old dance song by the Pointer Sisters. The older people had cleared the dance floor, and a younger group had taken over. Syneda was among them and motioned to Lorren.

"Go on, Lorren," Mama Nora said, laughing. "Of all my children, you and Syneda were the two who really liked to boogie-woogie."

Lorren laughed. She remembered how she and Syneda had constantly practiced their dance routines, waiting anxiously for the day they would receive a call to audition for "Soul Train." Of course, that had been wishful thinking on their part. "I think I will." She left to join her friends on the dance floor.

Justin's breath caught in his throat when Lorren began swaying her hips to the music. Her shoulders dipped and rolled while keeping time with the beat. Thoroughly enjoying herself, she laughed loudly and exuberantly with the others. Her legs were moving, and her feet were effortlessly flying through the intricate steps. It amazed him that she didn't appear to be working up any kind of sweat as her body gyrated to the exhilarating beat.

He was entranced. She didn't have to sweat; he was doing enough for both just watching her. He wiped perspiration from his forehead.

"That child's got rhythm, doesn't she?" Mama Nora smiled warmly at him.

Justin didn't have to ask Ms. Nora whom she was talking about. He wondered if his interest in Lorren was apparent to the older woman. "Yes, ma'am. She, uh, moves very well." His mind swam with images of Lorren's rhythmic movements in his bed. He could only imagine what she would feel like moving beneath him.

The dance ended and everyone clapped and cheered.

The song the DJ played next was a slow number by Janet Jackson. Justin felt a sudden need to feel Lorren in his arms, following his lead. "Excuse me, Ms. Nora."

Lorren, breathless from dancing, glanced in Justin's direction and saw him coming toward her. The little bit of breath she had left was lost. Even the air held still for his approach. He appeared to be clad in an aura of tightly reined sexuality she didn't know could exist in a man.

Until now.

Dear heaven, I have to get away from him. I can't allow myself to become attracted to him.

She quickly turned to Syneda. "Do me a favor and call me a cab."

"What? You're leaving? Now?"

"Yeah."

Syneda saw Justin approaching. "The brother has really gotten next to you, hasn't he?"

Lorren didn't pretend not to know to whom Syneda was referring. "Yeah, and I can't...I just can't deal with it now."

"It's been a year since your divorce, Lorren. When will you be able to deal with Justin Madaris, or any man for that matter?"

"I don't know, Syneda. I really don't know." She turned and hurried out the door.

Justin stopped his approach and watched Lorren walk out the door. That was the second time tonight she'd deliberately avoided him, and he was contemplating going after her.

He was incredulous. The desire to chase after a woman—any woman—had never come over him before. But then, he'd never before encountered a woman with the ability to send fire coursing through his veins, or one who made him feel so stimulated.

Not even Denise had done that.

His hand closed over the coin medallion nestled on his chest. He could feel it through the soft material of his shirt. Denise had given the gold chain from which hung a gold coin to him on their wedding night, and he'd worn it constantly, seeing no reason to take it off—even after her death. It was a visible, tangible sign of the strong love the two of them had shared, and the commitment they'd made. He had loved her with every breath in his body.

Over the years, he'd met and dated a number of attractive women, women who'd tempted his passions but hadn't been able to tangle his emotions. His thoughts shifted back to Lorren. Tonight she had done exactly that.

He frowned. The last thing he needed after years of striving for inner peace, of pushing away painful memories, was to become involved with a bitter woman consumed in disappointment and heartache over a broken marriage. A cynical, frustrated woman who could become a threat to the harmonious niche he'd created for himself since Denise's death.

It was obvious Lorren had locked her feelings away from any man who dared to get close. The moment he'd suggested they go out, the expression on her face had been anxious, almost stricken. He resented her ability to reawaken his protective instincts. After she'd told him of her views on love and marriage, he had wanted to find her ex-husband and do the man in. He must have been some kind of a jerk.

Justin sighed deeply. Some inexplicable need made dismissing her from his mind totally impossible. Lorren Jacobs was a puzzle, one he wanted to solve. In order to do that, he'd have to see her again. And he intended to do just that.

* * *

Lorren felt exhausted during the cab ride.

Her concentration turned to the darkened countryside beyond the car window. The cab's headlights occasionally shone on the huge signs along the interstate denoting the Bluebonnet Trails.

Four well-marked trails covering approximately forty miles of good, all-weather roads had been laid out years ago by the Ennis Garden Club. The vast fields of bluebonnets had been slowly disappearing as a result of the growth of the cattle industry. The trails were intended to preserve bluebonnets for future generations to enjoy. No section of the state had broader acres or wider expanses of bluebonnets than the countryside surrounding Ennis. She smiled, remembering her bicycle rides on the trails each spring.

"Here you are, lady." The rough voice of the cabdriver interrupted her thoughts.

"Thanks." She paid her fare and was glad she'd left quite a few outside lights burning. Only five houses surrounded Elliot Lake on the outskirts of town, between Dallas and Ennis. Mama Nora owned the lake house Lorren would be occupying. The other owners were out-of-towners who usually came to the lake only during the heat of the summer months.

According to Mama Nora, the son of the owners of the house next to hers was currently occupying it. Lorren hadn't seen any sign of anyone when she'd arrived earlier in the day.

Before she could step out of the vehicle, bright

headlights shone through the back window of the cab. A car had pulled off the main road and onto the single lane leading toward the lake houses.

"Expecting someone, miss?" the cabdriver asked when he noticed her hesitation in getting out of his cab.

Lorren welcomed the concern in his voice. "No, but since this is the only road to the lake, it's probably my neighbor coming home. But still, I'd appreciate it if you didn't leave just yet."

"No problem. I have a granddaughter about your age. I worry about her comings and goings all the time. We're living in dangerous times. Places aren't safe like they used to be. Why would you want to be out this far by yourself anyway? There's nothing around here but woods. The closest store is the Davises' gas station five miles back."

Lorren sighed. Mama Nora had asked her the same thing. "I want privacy."

"Well, you sure got it out here."

The sound of a car's engine came closer, and, moments later, a candy apple red Corvette pulled up beside the cab.

"Oh, that's the doctor, miss. You're safe. Good night."

A funny feeling settled in the pit of Lorren's stomach. "The doctor?"

"Yeah. He's been in town almost a year now and…"

The man's last words were lost on Lorren as she quickly exited from the cab. Her anger had reached its boiling point. The nerve of Justin Madaris following her home. Well, it was time to throw down on the brother, who at that moment was getting out of the sports car.

Lorren watched as the cab pulled off, leaving her and Justin alone. She turned to face him, totally ticked off. "Is there a reason you followed me, Dr. Madaris?"

"I didn't follow you, Lorren."

She glared up at him. "What are you talking about? If you didn't follow me, then why're you here?"

A smile tilted Justin's lips. "I live in the lake house through the trees. I'm your neighbor."

Chapter 2

Justin's statement rendered Lorren speechless. *He was her neighbor? He lived a stone's throw from her house?*

"My neighbor!" she exclaimed as a cloud of anxiety swept over her, and her power of speech returned. "Is this supposed to be a joke?"

Justin gave her a huge smile. "No, ma'am. I thought you knew."

Lorren frowned. "There's no way you could have thought that. And just how long have you known?"

Justin shrugged. "I've known for a week or so that someone would be occupying Ms. Nora's lake house. I only found out tonight it was you."

She lifted a dark brow. "Exactly when tonight?"

"Moments after you left the party. I think Ms. Nora was under the impression we both knew already."

Lorren tried remembering her conversation with Mama Nora when she'd asked to stay at the lake house. Mama Nora had said the oldest son of the owners was occupying the lake house next to hers, and he had moved to Ennis almost a year ago. Mama Nora *had* mentioned the man was a doctor in town. Hell's bells! How could she have forgotten that?

"Lorren, are you all right?"

Tilting her head back, she looked up at him. "Yes, I'm fine," she replied. "I'm just surprised."

"So was I when Ms. Nora told me. She's worried about you being out here alone. I told her I'd keep an eye out for you."

Lorren's chin raised to a stubborn slant. "You may be my neighbor, but you aren't my keeper. Do try remembering that. Good night, Dr. Madaris."

"If you'd give me the key, I'll open the door for you."

"I can do it myself."

Justin leaned back against the wood column fronting the lake house. "Just trying to be neighborly."

Lorren didn't know if it was the key not cooperating or the fact she couldn't get her fingers to relax, but the door lock wouldn't budge. When seconds ticked into minutes, she realized the futility of the situation. However, she was determined not to ask Justin for help even if she had to stay out there till morning.

"Here, let me try." Not giving her a chance to step

aside, Justin's arms slid around her to the door, where the key was partially inserted inside the lock.

Lorren could feel the hardness of Justin's chest pressed against her back. His closeness overwhelmed her, and the clean manly scent of him caused her flesh to tingle. The feel of his heated breath on her neck made a pulsing knot form in her stomach.

For crying out loud. I've never experienced anything like this before in my life! What in the name of heaven is happening to me?

"There you go. You may want to get that lock changed. It's kind of old."

Lorren swallowed deeply when Justin stepped back to give her the space she needed to turn around. She did so slowly. Feeling his gaze on her face, she refused to lift her head to meet it. At least not until she felt a little less shaky, and until the tremors quivering inside of her wouldn't affect her voice.

Justin stared at Lorren, trying to cope with the feelings engulfing him from her closeness. He became enmeshed in memories of them dancing together, of him holding her in his arms, his hands wrapped around her waist, and their bodies moving slowly to the music. He also remembered her dancing with her friends on the dance floor. And how the black silk material of her dress clung to her body with every movement.

His voice was thick and unsteady when he spoke. "Do you want me to check inside to make sure everything's okay before you go in?"

"That won't be necessary."

"All right." Justin's gaze held hers, then dropped to her mouth, a mouth freshly moistened by the nervous sweep of her tongue. His muscles clenched. Heat raced through him as he tried to retain a hold on his sanity. His gaze returned to her eyes. That same electrical shock of awareness he'd experienced twice at the party hit him full force.

Lorren watched him, unsure of his next move as he stood silhouetted under the porch lights. He took a step that brought him closer to her. Automatically, she took a step back. "It's late, Justin. I'm going inside."

"Don't forget, I'm next door if you need anything. No matter how late it is."

Eyes hooded, Lorren pursed her lips and nodded before taking another step backward into the house. "Good night, Justin."

"Good night." He turned and walked away as she closed the door.

Lorren leaned against the door and closed her eyes. Emotional turmoil churned through her. This was not supposed to be happening. She'd been in town less than twenty-four hours, and already she had met a man who could turn her life topsy-turvy and become a threat to the placid existence she'd planned for herself in Ennis.

And if that didn't beat all, he was her neighbor. Her closest and *only* neighbor…for miles. She drew in a long breath, feeling tears trickle down her cheeks. She hadn't cried since that day in the judge's chamber almost a year ago. It had been the day her marriage to Scott had ended.

The tears hadn't been for the finality of her marriage; she'd been overjoyed about that. They had been for the cruel words Scott had leveled at her in the presence of the judge and their attorneys. He'd informed her he was glad to be rid of her since she had never been able to perform the natural womanly function of a wife during their marriage.

She would never forget the quick look that had passed between the other three men before the judge warned Scott against any further outburst. It had been the most humiliating day of her life. Scott had succeeded in degrading her until the very end.

Lorren slowly opened her eyes. She was too tired, both mentally and physically, to relive memories of her past or to begin pondering her future. At the moment, all she wanted was to forget about everything and go to bed.

Wiping the tears from her eyes, she straightened and went into the bedroom.

Intrusive bright sunlight flooded the bedroom, awakening Lorren. Shifting her head on the pillow, she gazed up at the ceiling. Unfortunately for her, sleep hadn't come easily. Long after going to bed last night, she'd tossed and turned. The room had been naturally cooled by the breeze blowing off the lake through the window, but her body had been hot and restless. She had been acutely aware of every inch of her naked skin left bare by the skimpy gown she'd worn to bed.

How was one man capable of making her feel things in the space of a few hours when Scott hadn't made her feel anything during the two years they'd been married? In the beginning she'd been attracted to Scott, or so she'd thought. But this attraction she felt toward Justin Madaris was completely different. And it scared her to death.

Sighing, she threw back the bedcovers and reached for her bathrobe. Putting it on, she belted it firmly around her waist and headed for the bathroom.

A little while later, she stepped into the shower. Hot water rushed through her lathered hair, soaking her brown skin. Closing her eyes, she relished the feel of it streaming over her. Turning her face into the spray, she let the shampoo's foam slide down her back, thighs, and legs. She felt a warm glow inside her body as she remembered the feel of Justin's hard, muscular chest pressed against the curve of her back and the roundness of her bottom when he'd opened the door for her last night.

Adjusting the showerhead to release a lighter spray, Lorren threw her head back, arching her neck against the flow of water, liking the feel of it wetting her lips.

Then the unimaginable happened.

Her mind conjured up a mental image of Justin in the shower with her, placing light kisses on her lips and softly caressing her back and shoulders, and the tender skin between her breasts.

The depth of Lorren's sensual mental diversion startled her back to reality. She snapped her eyes open. *For Pete's sake! What's happening to me?* Turning off the water, she quickly stepped out of the shower and hurriedly dried herself with a thick velour towel.

First last night, and now this. It's bad enough being isolated out here with the man, without starting to have sexual fantasies about him. Girl, you better get your act together.

Stepping into her robe, she tightened the sash at the waist just as the doorbell chimed. She walked out of the bathroom to the living room.

"Who is it?" she asked, peering through the tiny glass peephole in the door. A hot ache grew in her throat. The flaps of a shirt gaped open and a dark, muscular, hair-covered chest dominated her view. She sucked in a quick breath. It was as if her fantasies had zapped Justin to her doorstep.

"It's me Lorren, Justin."

Lorren reached a trembling hand for the doorknob. Her palms became sweaty. Her mouth felt dry. Slowly, she opened the door.

Justin stood before her dressed in a pair of outlandishly sexy swimming shorts and a camp shirt. Somehow she managed to speak. "What do you want, Justin?"

Justin's gaze swept over Lorren. Even with her hair damp from a recent shower and her face scrubbed clean of makeup, she was breathtaking.

He would bet the keys to his Vette she wasn't wearing anything under her robe. X-ray vision was something he'd give just about anything to have at the moment.

"Good morning, Lorren. I happened to be in the neighborhood," he teased as a smile touched his lips, "and was wondering if you'd like to join me in an early morning swim?"

Lorren looked at him, trying not to notice how the hair on his chest tapered down his sides, spreading out again along his navel until it disappeared beneath the waistband of his shorts. She marveled at the splendor of his trim flanks and long muscular legs. There wasn't an ounce of spare flesh on him.

"I—I can't," she stuttered, forcing her gaze from his body to his eyes.

Justin smiled. "What is it you can't do? You can't join me, or you can't swim?"

"I—I can't join you because I haven't had breakfast yet," Lorren answered, her tongue stumbling over the first excuse she could think of.

Justin's eyes twinkled. "Never fear, the doctor's here." From behind him, he produced a bag. "It occurred to me, since you'd just arrived yesterday, you hadn't had a chance to go to the grocery store. So being the friendly and considerate neighbor that I am, I decided breakfast would be my treat to officially welcome you to the neighborhood. With your permission, I plan to take your kitchen by storm."

Lorren had a feeling that wasn't the only thing he

would take by storm if given the chance. Common sense told her to refuse his generosity. However, it suddenly dawned on her that common sense was something she seemed to lack around him.

Whether she liked it or not, he *was* living next door, so she might as well follow his lead and try to be neighborly. Besides, she really was hungry. "How can I reject such an offer?" she said, stepping aside.

A subtle hint of pure male, and the crisp, clean scent of aftershave, permeated the air as Justin swept past Lorren. He turned to face her, his gaze moving from the top of her damp head to the polished toes of her bare feet peeking from under her robe. His gaze slowly retraced its path. "I'll fix the main course."

Lorren nodded. "All right. And I'll make the coffee. I noticed a full can last night."

Justin followed Lorren into the kitchen. She tried to concentrate on taking the cups out of the cabinet. Spinning around and colliding with the hard wall of his chest, she slowly lifted her gaze to his. There was something about his features she hadn't noticed last night. His sculptured cheekbones added a greater dimension to his already dark handsome face.

"Sorry. I didn't realize you were so close," she said, swallowing hard. She turned to the sink to pour water in the coffeemaker. Even with her back to Justin, she was aware of his blatant scrutiny.

"Did you get a good night's sleep?" he asked.

Lorren turned around. "Yes," she lied. "What about you?"

"Best sleep I've had in a long time."

"Glad to hear it. Now, if you'll excuse me, I'm going to get dressed."

Justin blocked her way out of the kitchen and made no attempt to step aside. "Why? I like what you're wearing. The color peach looks good on you."

Lorren looked down at her robe. Although the thick material hid a lot from Justin's eyes, it wasn't the proper thing to wear when entertaining a male guest.

"Thanks, but I like the color I'm changing into even better," she said. "I'll be back in a minute. If you need anything while I'm gone, check inside the cabinets or the closet." She walked around him and out of the kitchen to the bedroom.

Lorren was slightly unsettled getting dressed. After blow-drying her hair and applying light makeup, she headed back to the kitchen. The rich aroma of eggs and bacon filled the air.

She paused at the kitchen's entrance. Justin had evidently searched the place and found a hand-crocheted cotton lace tablecloth. The table was set and there was also a beautiful bouquet of bluebonnets for the centerpiece. He was leaning over the stove, tending to a tray of pancakes.

She was amazed. "I wasn't gone that long. How in the world did you accomplish all this in that short time?"

A gleam shone in Justin's eyes. "I work fast. I don't believe in beating around the bush or taking things slow."

Lorren knew he was talking about more than his cooking abilities. "Well, your swiftness at getting things done is appreciated this morning. I'm starving." She crossed the room to the counter.

Justin's gaze followed her movement. The soft material of her blue romper did more than hint at the feminine curves it covered. He watched her hips sway provocatively with each step, enticing him with an allure that was as old as mankind. She turned around to face him.

"How do you like it?"

Justin blinked twice. He swallowed hard. "Excuse me?" he asked huskily.

"Your coffee. How do you like it? Or should I ask, how do you take it?"

He cleared his throat and said the first words that came to his muddled mind. "Black and hot."

"What?" Lorren stared at him dumbfounded.

"Oh, I meant black with sugar. Sorry."

Lorren poured the steaming hot liquid into a cup, then added a spoon of sugar. Walking over to him, she handed him the cup, careful to avoid touching him. It was bad enough keeping her gaze from roaming over his physique.

"Thanks." His gaze scanned her outfit. "I take it you've decided not to go swimming with me this morning," he said, disappointed.

"Afraid so. I still have a lot of unpacking to do. I hope that doesn't mean you won't be feeding me after all."

Justin laughed. "No, but it does mean you owe me a rain check."

"I told you last night, I don't give rain checks," she said, smiling, and finding herself relaxing in his company in spite of her apprehensions.

Justin smiled. "Then I'll be your first." He gave her a teasing wink. "Come on, let's eat."

Lorren eagerly escaped to the table and sat down. Justin sat across from her and began spooning hefty servings of scrambled eggs, bacon, and pancakes onto her plate.

"Thanks." Lorren dug hungrily into the meal. "Justin, this is wonderful. I haven't eaten food that tasted this good in a long time. You're definitely full of surprises."

Justin watched as she parted her lips and small white teeth bit down on a piece of crisp bacon. Slowly, she chewed the piece of meat, savoring the taste. A crumb clung to the corner of her mouth. A knot rose in his throat. He was tempted to sweep the crumb away with his tongue.

"Who taught you how to cook, Justin?"

Justin shifted in his chair as he experienced a tremor in his stomach—well, not quite in his stomach. Actually, it was a little lower. He took a calming breath before answering her. "I'm the oldest of six kids, so I was the one who had to learn everything. I enjoyed helping my mom in the kitchen as much as I enjoyed performing surgery on my sisters' baby dolls."

Lorren couldn't keep the amusement out of her voice. "You didn't really do that to their dolls, did you?"

He chuckled. "Afraid so. It got so bad they would hide them from me. I tried convincing them I was just making the dolls better, but after a while, they didn't buy it." He laughed. "I grew out of it when my parents started using my allowance to buy new dolls."

She smiled. "So you always knew you wanted to be a doctor?"

"Yes, I think so. I've always cared for people and wanted to help others. What about you? Did you always want to become a writer?"

"No," she replied softly, remembering the first story she'd written at the age of nine. "After my parents' death, the courts assigned Mama Nora and Papa Paul as my foster parents. At first it was quite an adjustment for me, and I wanted to be left alone. Mama Nora discovered I liked to read and gave me a lot of books to occupy my time. Soon I was writing my own stories. I would give them to her for safekeeping, not knowing of her plans to submit them to a publisher when I got older. She did, and in addition to becoming a published author, I received a four-year scholarship to attend college in California. I've been writing ever since. My books are specifically designed and written to commemorate our ethnic heritage, as well as to entertain and enlighten children."

Justin nodded. He wondered how her parents

had died, but didn't want to ask her about it. He of all people knew how hard it was losing a loved one. In her case, she had lost two. But she'd still made something of her life. He was impressed. "That's quite a success story."

"You think so?" Lorren's voice clearly reflected her surprise with Justin's comment.

"Of course, don't you?"

It had been a long time since she'd considered any part of her life as being successful. The guilt of a failed marriage had overshadowed any such thoughts. But now, hearing Justin's words made a part of her feel good inside. "I guess I don't think about it. Writing stories is something I enjoy doing."

Justin knew he was probably about to tread on dangerous ground with his next question. "Did you meet your husband in California?"

Justin's question brought back memories of the day she and Scott had met. It had been one morning in a small café across the street from the newspaper publisher where she worked. Having graduated from college only a few months earlier and landed her first job as an editorial assistant, she'd been experiencing her first real taste of independence.

The first things she'd noticed about Scott were how handsome, well dressed, and sophisticated he was. Three years older than her, he worked as a project consultant for a major television network. For their first date, he'd taken her to an elegant restaurant in LA. On all their other dates, he'd made her feel special and important…and loved.

Scott had pursued her for more than six months before finally accepting that she would not agree to sleep with him or any man before marriage. Not engaging in premarital sex was a decision she'd made years earlier because of the good Christian upbringing Mama Nora had given her. But that decision had been reinforced after seeing what Syneda had gone through.

Syneda's father never married her mother, and, knowing she was dying of breast cancer, Ms. Walters had written to the man who had fathered her child, asking that he come and get their ten-year-old daughter and provide a home for her. Syneda's mom, who had never stopped loving the man, had died believing he would come. She had also convinced Syneda that the father she never knew would come for her, thus giving Syneda something to look forward to. Syneda's father never came.

Even believing that Scott actually loved her had not been enough to change Lorren's mind about sleeping with him before marriage. At first, he had continued to hound her about it, but on that issue she had stood her ground.

It was only after her marriage to Scott, which came exactly eight months to the day after they'd met, that Lorren discovered just how self-centered, overambitious, and controlling he was. After she had thoroughly disappointed him in bed on their wedding night, he'd been bent on making her life with him miserable.

But he would keep her anyway, he'd told her, and had further elaborated that he believed in time she could develop technique and finesse a little more to his liking. Besides, he'd added, even with her shortcomings in the bedroom, she had other things going for her—looks and a promising career.

It didn't take her long to realize that he really didn't need a wife, but a hostess for when he entertained his colleagues and associates. He'd told her countless times it was her duty as his wife to help advance his career.

The only reason she'd stayed with him those two years, aside from her deep belief in their commitment, was that she hadn't wanted to be a failure by giving up on their marriage or on him.

In the end, all she'd gotten out of her marriage with Scott was the stripping away of her pride and confidence. That was the price she'd paid for loving him.

Bringing her thoughts back to the present, Lorren responded to Justin's question. "Yes, I met my ex-husband there." She quickly changed the subject, not wanting to talk to Justin about Scott.

"What brought you to a small town like Ennis? I would think this place is rather boring to someone from Houston."

Taking the hint she didn't want to discuss her ex-husband, Justin answered, "I'd lived in a big city all my life and wanted to try a small town." He smiled.

"Senator Malone and my father attended Morehouse together, and when Ms. Nora told him about Dr. Powers's retirement, and that the town was in need of a general practitioner, he contacted me to see if I was interested."

A wry smile curled up the corners of Lorren's mouth. She could just imagine the single women's reaction to the town's new doctor. Especially one as handsome as Justin. Her smile faded when she remembered all the pain she'd endured after being taken in by a handsome face. She was determined not to get sucked into that kind of hurt and heartbreak again.

"I feel stuffed. Breakfast was really good. Thanks." She stood and began clearing the table.

Justin picked up on the sudden change in her. She acted as if she was in a hurry for him to leave. For some reason, the amiable time between them had ended. "I'll help with the dishes."

She shook her head. "There's no need. I'm probably one of the few women alive who enjoys doing dishes. When I lived with Mama Nora, I used to make money off the other kids when it was their week for kitchen duty."

Justin grinned. "As much as I like cooking, I've never developed a fondness for washing dishes. And washing pots is really the pits." He stood. "At least let me help you clear the table."

The two of them removed the dishes from the table, then Justin took his leave. As they approached the front door, he asked, "Are you sure you won't change your mind about going swimming?"

"Yes, I'm sure."

Justin studied her face for a moment. "How about dinner tonight? I know of this swell restaurant in Dallas that serves wonderful seafood. Then afterward I can take you dancing. There's this nice—"

"Justin, I won't go out with you." Lorren paused as she formulated her words. "It was fun sharing breakfast with you, but I don't think we should overdo it."

Justin rested against the closed door. "What do you mean?"

"We shouldn't make it a habit, spending a lot of time together. The fewer personal things are between us, the better off we'll both be. We're like oil and water. We don't mix. I'm a realist and you're a dreamer."

"Why? Because I believe in fate?"

"Yes, which means you probably believe there's a pot of gold at the end of the rainbow. You think every marriage should be like the one you had—made in heaven. I found out the hard way that's not true. No one gets married expecting doom, but it happens to the best of us. Unfortunately, statistics have proved it happens to most. I believe true love and a happy marriage are things only shared by a select few."

"I happen to disagree with that assessment," Justin replied, his voice low and sexy. "Sounds like you have a case of divorcitis," he said, smiling mischievously, daring her to smile with him. Reluctantly, she did.

Lorren wondered what there was about Justin that made just looking at him pleasurable, notwithstanding the ability to send her emotions into overdrive. "Divorcitis? Oh my gosh, Doctor. What's that?" she asked teasingly, sounding like a frantic patient.

The soothing rays of the early morning sun came through the window and shone on Lorren's face, giving it a velvety brown softness. Justin thought she looked even more beautiful than last night. He cleared his throat and spoke in a professional tone. "It's a condition that plagues divorcees when, for whatever reason, they refuse to accept the fact there's life after a divorce. They seem to equate a divorce decree with a death decree. And you, Lorren Jacobs, have the usual symptoms."

Lorren decided not to tell him a death decree was not what she equated with her divorce. She'd considered her divorce a rebirth. "I gather a loss of appetite isn't one of the symptoms," she said, laughing at the ridiculousness of their conversation.

Justin grinned. "Nope, your appetite isn't affected; however, at times your peace of mind is. Since I've diagnosed your condition, and free of charge I might add, I don't want to waste any time before starting to treat you. Time is of the utmost importance when handling a condition like yours."

"You don't say, Doc?"

"Oh, I do say," he assured her with a smooth smile. "To leave it untreated could be detrimental to your well-being. However, when given the proper attention, the prognosis is excellent. And with the right dosage of tender, loving care, you'll be good as new in no time."

Lorren's laugh was soft. "Good as new? Really?"

Justin's smile widened. "Yeah, really."

"And just who'll be giving me this TLC?"

"I will."

"Ummm. To be on the safe side, maybe I should obtain a second opinion."

He leaned toward her. "A second opinion in your case isn't necessary. I'm the only one who can diagnose your condition. And more importantly, I'm the only one with a cure. I'll start you off with a mild dosage," he said, his mouth inches from hers, "and when I think you're ready for something stronger, I'll see that you get it."

Lorren felt her heart skip a beat. Was Justin going to kiss her? Did she want him to? No! She had to keep her head on straight. But he had the most sensuous mouth. What would his lips feel like on hers?

She crushed the thought and stepped back. "I think we've played this game long enough, Justin. Weren't you about to leave?"

Justin moved, closing the distance between them, He was so close, the tips of his shoes touched the tips of her flats. "I've changed my mind."

His voice had deepened and thickened. "I want

to do something I could barely refrain from doing last night."

Justin's lips brushed against hers as he spoke.

A wild shudder of pleasure touched Lorren's body. Blood coursed through her veins like a raging river. Succumbing to curiosity and the attraction she had fought since first meeting him, her lips parted.

A groan rumbled in Justin's throat as he closed his mouth over hers. He made sure his kiss was gentle, yet seductive. Her taste was sweet, hot, sensuous. He hungered for her and relentlessly explored her mouth, demanding a response and enticing her tongue to mate with his.

Not only was he kissing her, Lorren thought, but he was encouraging her to participate, something Scott never did. He'd said hugging, kissing, and caressing weren't a necessary part of lovemaking.

Heat throbbed deep within Lorren as Justin's thrusting tongue dueled with hers in a slow, sensual motion. She wound her arms around his neck and arched against him, quivering, as hot waves of desire consumed her. Sliding her hands over his rib cage, she felt the hardness of his muscled body through the material of his clothing.

This was better than anything she had ever experienced before. The times she and Scott had kissed had never excited her this way, so completely, so thoroughly.

Her senses pulsated with the strength, feel, and scent of Justin. These new sensations stirred passion, the likes of which she'd never known, to rage within her. Operating purely on instinct, her body leaned into him, intensifying the kiss as she slanted her mouth against his.

Lorren's barrier of self-protectiveness should have had her turning from any intimate contact with a man. Instead, she automatically rose on tiptoe to follow Justin's mouth when he unexpectedly pulled away.

With a fevered moan Justin lifted his mouth from Lorren's to draw much-needed air into his lungs. "I can't handle too much more of this," he whispered roughly, burying his face in her neck and breathing a kiss there. "I just knew it would be like this. I just knew we'd be good together."

His words zapped Lorren back to reality. No! They wouldn't be good together. After what had just happened between them, there was no doubt in her mind he'd be better than good. But she knew with that same certainty, she'd be a disappointment to him. How could she have forgotten that one elemental fact about herself?

Suddenly anxious to escape his presence, she twisted out of his arms, taking a deep breath. "I'm sorry if I gave you the wrong impression, Justin, but I don't sleep around."

Justin's eyes grazed a path from Lorren's swollen lips to the stubborn set of her chin. The woman had transformed the act of kissing into a work of art. At the beginning she'd seemed unsure of what to do, which he'd found strange for someone who'd been married before. But in no time at all she had him indulging in pleasure so wonderful, it felt almost sinful. She had enjoyed their kiss just as much as he had. But he had picked up on the fact that what he'd seen in her eyes was more surprise at the effects of the kiss than recognition of the results of it. If he didn't know better, he'd think she had never been properly kissed before.

"And I don't sleep around either, Lorren," he said quietly. "As a doctor, I know just how rampant AIDS is. I'm a firm believer you should think twice before going to bed with just anyone." He took a step forward. "While I don't go in for one-night stands, I don't have anything against an affair."

A lean, dark finger caressed her cheek. There was such an awe-inspiring beauty about her, with her mouth slightly swollen from his kiss and her face tinted with desire. "I think we may be headed for one," he said softly.

"No." The response was fast from Lorren's lips.

Justin's reply was even quicker. "Yes." His dark eyes held hers. "You're attracted to me just as much as I am to you, whether you're willing to admit it or not. Think about it."

"There's nothing to think about," she replied curtly.

"I believe differently."

Turning, he walked out the door.

Chapter 3

"Why do men think they know everything?" Lorren asked Syneda as they sat at a table in Sophie's Diner.

Syneda looked up from her meal. "I guess it's a man thing." She raised a brow. "Is there a particular reason for this little episode of male-bashing? You've been on a roll since we got here."

Lorren took a sip of her soft drink, then regarded her friend through lowered lashes. "No reason."

The look Syneda sent her was pointed. "Let's not get cutesy, Lorren Nicole Jacobs. We've been through too much together. The disappointment of my father not coming for me, your schoolgirl infatuation with Carlos Nottenkamper, and last, but not least, your bummer of a marriage to Scott."

Lorren raised her eyes heavenward. "Thanks for reminding me of that last one."

Syneda smiled sweetly. "Couldn't pass up the chance. So, are you going to tell me what's bothering you, or will you keep me guessing?"

Lorren tried pulling her scattered emotions together. When she spoke, her voice was low and unsteady. "I'm attracted to Justin Madaris."

"For crying out loud, Lorren. Tell me something I don't know. Have you forgotten that I'm the one who called a cab for you the other night. It was obvious at Mama Nora's party the two of you were attracted to each other."

Lorren shook her head. "No, Syneda. You don't understand. I mean *deeply* attracted, to the point that I've felt things." She dropped her voice lower, her words barely more than a ragged whisper. "Physical things."

Syneda stared at her friend for a moment. She would have grinned at the bewildered expression on Lorren's face had she not known the depth of her anxiety. "Oh, Lorren," she said softly, a tender smile dancing across her lips. "Honey, you're supposed to feel physical things when you're attracted to someone."

"I didn't feel anything physical like this for Scott."

Syneda sighed. "Then *that* should tell you something, shouldn't it? When will you realize that Scott Howard didn't walk on water? In my opinion, he didn't walk on land either. He crawled around on his belly like other snakes." She smiled. "So, you're really attracted to the good doctor, uh? Well, hallelujah! It's about time you're attracted to someone. Now maybe you'll stop overprotecting yourself because of what Scott put you through and get on with your life."

"You act as though I haven't dated at all since my divorce. I've gone out with numerous men."

"Numerous men?" Syneda asked, drawing out the words slowly. "Don't make me get hysterical. What you dated were numerous wimps. The only competition you got was from their mamas. Face it, honey, Justin Madaris is no wimp."

Placing her elbows on the table, Syneda laced her fingers under her chin. "Why are you fighting your attraction to Justin, Lorren?"

Lorren took a deep breath before answering. Syneda was one of the few people who knew most of the details of her breakup with Scott. "You know Scott's accusations. You know all the things he said about me."

"Yes," Syneda answered softly. "And I've told you a million times not to believe any of it. He said those things to hurt you. Hurting you was the only way he could cover his own feelings of inadequacy."

Lorren took another sip of her drink before responding. "I really wish I could believe that."

A wry smile tilted the corners of Syneda's mouth. "Do more than believe it, Lorren. You can prove Scott was wrong."

Lorren's brow shot up. "And how am I supposed to do that?"

"You know the answer to that. The way I see it," Syneda continued, "there's only one thing left for you to do. Sleep with Justin."

Lorren's mouth dropped open at the calm, easy way Syneda had made the suggestion. "Syneda Tremain Walters! Are you out of your cotton-pickin' mind?"

"No, but you'll be if you don't make an attempt to find out the truth once and for all. So what's the problem?"

Lorren glanced at her friend sharply, wondering if the onion burger Syneda had just eaten had gone to her head instead of her stomach. Syneda didn't believe in casual sex any more than she did. "For your information, Syneda, Justin Madaris *is* the problem. He's not the type of man I want to get involved with. It's bad enough he's my neighbor, but I simply refuse to let—"

"Whoa, whoa, whoa. Back up a minute. Did you just say Justin's your neighbor?"

Lorren shifted uneasily in her seat. "Yeah, but that doesn't—"

"Hold it right there. Let me get this straight, girlfriend. Justin's out there with you, all alone, in no-man's-land?"

"It's not no-man's-land."

Syneda gave her a half smile. "All right, all right,

so it isn't no-man's-land. The two of you are out there all alone in the boondocks?"

Lorren raised her eyes to the ceiling. "Evidently there's a point to all of this. If so, please make it."

"The point is, I think Justin Madaris is exactly what you need, a man with experience."

"Syneda, a man with experience is the last thing I need. His expectations would be too high. I couldn't handle it if another man was to tell me how worthless I am in bed."

Smiling through the sadness she felt for her friend, Syneda said, "As far as I'm concerned, the person who told you that lie wasn't a man, but a snake. Now tell me, what have you and Justin been doing out there all alone?"

Lorren took another sip of her drink. She hadn't seen Justin since the morning he had prepared breakfast for her. That had been two days ago. She'd expected him to show up uninvited again with the pretense of wanting to go swimming, or being a good neighbor by checking up on her. When he didn't, she'd become confused at her mixed feelings of both relief and disappointment.

"We haven't been doing anything," she finally replied. "I haven't seen him much."

"Well, don't look now, but the good doctor just walked through the door. He's seen us and is headed this way. My-oh-my, it should be against the law what that man does to a pair of Levi's jeans."

When Lorren turned to look at Justin, she had the

irrational urge to bolt out the door. She felt trapped, and a shiver swept down her spine. The mere sight of him did strange things to her.

"Good afternoon," Justin greeted, stopping at their table.

"Justin, what a pleasant surprise. Come join us," Syneda said, a smile curving her lips.

He returned the smile. "Thanks." He sat down in the chair next to Lorren. A waitress came to take his order. "Hi, Sunnie. Just give me the usual."

Justin and Syneda went into a round of topics, ranging from the weather to foreign affairs. Lorren contributed to the conversation only when asked a direct question. For the most part she tried ignoring Justin's presence. However, every time his gaze lingered on her, she was reminded of his parting words to her the other day.

"We'd love to. Wouldn't we, Lorren?" Syneda asked.

Lorren blinked. "What? I'm sorry, I'm afraid I wasn't listening. My mind was elsewhere."

"Justin invited us to a cookout Thursday night, and I've accepted," Syneda said, giving her a meaningful look. "That will be great since that's when I'm staying overnight with you."

Lorren shrugged. "Fine."

The waitress reappeared at their table. Lorren and Syneda declined dessert, but Justin ordered a slice of strawberry shortcake.

"There's nothing like an onion burger from this

place to set you back. I'll probably have indigestion for weeks. Any good advice, Doctor?" Syneda asked, grinning.

Justin smiled. "A teaspoon of baking soda mixed with water. It's a homemade remedy that works."

"I'll give it a try," Syneda said before glancing at her watch. "Well, I hate to run, but I've got to go."

Lorren looked up startled. "Go where?"

"Shopping. But there's no reason for you to leave, too," she replied, with eyes twinkling in devilment.

Syneda turned to Justin. "Thanks for the invitation to the cookout."

Justin stood when Syneda got out of her chair. He smiled. "My pleasure, and don't worry about your bill. I'll take care of it for both you ladies."

"Thanks. That's kind of you. I'll see you guys later."

Lorren felt abandoned and thoroughly set up by her friend. Looking across the table, she found Justin's eyes on her as he sat back down.

"How have you been, Lorren?"

"Fine."

"Are you almost all settled in?"

"Not quite."

Justin held her gaze with his for a few moments. "So you decided to go swimming the other day after all." It was a statement, not a question.

Lorren's eyes widened. "How did you—" she began, then broke off as she realized what the only possible answer to her unfinished question could be. He'd been at home. "I, ah—"

"You what, Lorren?"

She hesitated before answering. "I didn't know you were home. Your car wasn't parked out front. I assumed you had gone somewhere."

Justin leaned back in his chair. A slow smile touched his features. He sensed her nervousness. "Most of the time I keep my Vette parked in the back, under a shed. Texas weather can be murder on a good paint job. And to answer the question you didn't complete, the reason I know you went swimming is because I saw you."

And what he'd seen had been a sight to behold. He'd been sitting at his kitchen table, which overlooked the lake, reading an informative but boring medical journal article. For some reason he'd glanced up and caught sight of her. Whatever information he'd been reading abruptly faded from his mind when he'd received the jolt of his life. Of course, he'd known she had a shapely figure. The black dress she'd worn at Ms. Nora's party had clearly emphasized that. But the swimming suit she'd been wearing had knocked the breath out of him. All he could do was stare. He couldn't pull his gaze from her. He had all but devoured the vision of her wet curvy body, admiring every inch of it.

Lorren shifted her chair. "I, ah—" she swallowed. "After you left, I changed my mind and thought the swim would relax me."

Justin studied Lorren's well-manicured hand tightening around the glass of soda. "Did it?"

Lorren lifted a brow. "Did it what?"

"Did the swim relax you?"

She shrugged. "Yeah, pretty much."

He smiled. "I'm glad."

Lorren's throat suddenly felt dry, and she took a huge swallow of soda. Justin seemed amused, not irritated, that she'd gone swimming alone, less than an hour after turning down his invitation to go swimming with him.

"You have nice strokes."

Lorren almost choked on her drink. "Excuse me?"

"Your strokes are nice. You're a good swimmer."

She studied him intently. "You must have seen a lot that day."

Smiling, his teeth flashed white against his dark skin. "Yeah," he said huskily. "I saw enough. And I was very impressed with everything I saw. Every bit of it."

Lorren bridled at the double entendre.

Before she could dissect his words, he bailed himself out. "With your swimming, of course." He grinned lazily, certain she knew her aquatic ability had nothing to do with his remarks.

"Of course," she returned stiffly.

"Have you given any thought to what I asked you the other day?"

He saw her tense at his question. Her eyes met

his candidly. "As I told you, there's nothing to think about." She stood. "Well, I'll be seeing ya."

"Where're you headed?"

"Fred's Garage. I had my car shipped here from California. It arrived this morning with a flat tire."

"Wait up and I'll walk with you partway," Justin said, signaling the waitress for the checks. "My next patient isn't due in the office until three."

Lorren glanced around the crowded diner, with its clinking dishes, faded wallpaper, and aromas of home-cooked meals. Over the years, it appeared very little had changed, including Sophie's clientele. There were still the truck drivers, senior citizens, and some of the younger locals who enjoyed Sophie's down-home country breakfast in the mornings, her mouthwatering lunch at noon, and her delectable soulful spread at dinnertime. Her sweet potato pie was worth dying for.

"Ready?" Justin broke into her thoughts.

"Yes. I really don't need an escort," she said to Justin when he ushered her out of the restaurant.

"I know, but I need to walk off lunch anyway."

They were both quiet as they strolled along the sidewalk. More than once she was drawn closer to his side in order to let people pass. And each time she was acutely aware of him holding his ground so their bodies would brush against each other.

Lorren tried concentrating on her surroundings. Some years ago the citizens of Ennis had decided to preserve their historic downtown. As a result, after extensive development, renovation, and restoration, the numerous buildings lining Main Street had undergone some degree of revitalization, preserving a bit of the historical nostalgia of her favorite part of town. It had become the central business district.

"Here we are," Lorren said, upon reaching Fred's Garage. "That's my car over there," she stated, pointing to the dark blue Camry. "It should be ready now. It's been here since this morning."

Justin nodded. "Even so, you'd better check to be sure. I've discovered punctuality and timely service aren't Fred's strong points."

Lorren couldn't help the smile creeping into her features. "You're right. I guess some things never change."

"And some things will in good time," he replied, his eyes fixed on her. The true meaning of his words was all too clear. "If your car isn't ready, let me know. I'll be glad to give you a lift home."

"Thanks, but that won't be necessary."

"How about going swimming with me this evening? The only patient I have is the one scheduled at three."

Lorren hooked her thumbs in the pockets of her jeans and met Justin's gaze. An idea began forming in her head. What if she agreed to become involved with him? Or at least let him think she had. How would he handle it if her preaffair requirements were more than he was willing to agree to? Would he suddenly back off? Was she brave enough to pull off such a stunt? The thought was insane, but if there was a possibility it might work and get him to leave her alone, then…

A huge smile appeared on Lorren's face. "I'd love to go swimming with you, Justin. I owe you a rain check anyway."

A look of surprise registered on Justin's chestnut features. "I thought you didn't give rain checks."

"You'll be my first."

He studied her, his eyes dark and intense. "Are you sure?"

She knew he was referring to more than just swimming. "Yes, I'm sure."

"Okay, then I'll see you later. I better get back to the office. Remember the offer still stands if you need a ride home."

"Thanks. I'll do that." Lorren watched as he turned to walk away, suddenly feeling in control. "Justin?" she called after him.

He turned around. "Yeah?"

With dazzling determination she decided she might as well go for the gusto. "Don't worry about dinner. It'll be my treat this evening after our swim," she said breezily. "It's the least I can do after your terrific breakfast."

He stared at her. "Thanks."

She watched him until he was no longer in sight.

Had she bitten off more than she could chew?

* * *

Upon arriving at the office, Justin discovered that Mrs. Breland, his three o'clock appointment, had canceled. Just as well, he thought. His mind was definitely not as focused as it should be. All his mental activity was concentrated on one person—Lorren Jacobs. The woman had him more confused than ever.

Why had she suddenly accepted his invitation to go swimming *and* invited him to dinner? Had she decided an affair with him wasn't such a bad idea? He had gone to bed last night thinking that a woman like Lorren was the last thing he needed in his life right now.

But the last thing he had been prepared for were dreams of her. The sweet image of her curvy body had tortured him in sleep. In his dreams he had tasted her, soothed her, and gently destroyed her defenses. But his torment hadn't stopped there. He'd also dreamed of holding her tightly in his arms as he made love to her, sinking deeper into her body, inhaling her fragrance as his body vibrated with a fever that…

There was a sudden knock on the door. He jumped at the sound. "Come in."

Sandra Dickerson, a middle-aged woman who doubled as both his receptionist and secretary, peeked around the half-opened door. "Your mom's on the line," she said, smiling. "And I'm out of here until morning."

"Have a good evening, Sandra. See you then."

"Okay, see ya," she said, waving and closing the door behind her.

Justin took a long steadying breath before picking up the phone on his desk. "Mom? When did you and Dad get back?" His parents, both college professors at a university in Houston, had been visiting friends in Atlanta for the past two weeks.

"We got back this morning and right in the nick of time. Dex called within twenty minutes after we returned."

Justin's smile widened at the mention of the brother he hadn't seen in quite some time. Dex was working in Australia as a geologist with a major oil company.

"How is he?"

Marilyn Madaris released an excited breath. "You'll find out soon enough. He'll be here for Christy's birthday party."

"Wonderful! Is he coming home to stay?"

"Let's hope so."

Justin heard the deep longing in his mother's voice. In his mind he could envision her, a Nancy Wilson look-alike, sitting at the kitchen table wearing a smile only mothers wore when they thought of their children returning home. He had seen that same motherly smile on Ms. Nora's face when she'd told him that Lorren was his neighbor.

"And how have you been, Justin?"

"Fine, Mom."

"Have you been seeing any nice girls lately, dear?"

Leave it to his mom not to beat around the bush

at anything, he thought with a smile. That was Marilyn Madaris's style. After a brief hesitation, he replied, absently fingering the medallion around his neck. "I do my share of dating."

"Really? As far as I'm concerned, they're all faceless women since your family hasn't met any of them. It's hard for a mother with three sons to accept the fact that none of them have marriage on their minds."

Justin grinned. "I'm sure you can forgive Dex for his lack of enthusiasm. His divorce from Caitlin nearly tore him apart. And you can definitely forget Clayton. He claims the only men that aren't fools are bachelors."

"Humph," she snorted. "And what about you?"

"I'd remarry in a heartbeat if the right woman came along, Mom, you know that," he chuckled.

"Do I, Justin? I'm beginning to think this fate song you've been singing over the years is for the birds. A part of me can't help but wonder if perhaps you're only fooling yourself."

"Fooling myself? About what?"

"About ever wanting to marry again."

Justin raised his eyes to the ceiling. "Mom, if it's meant for me to marry again, I will. Now tell me how the rest of the family is doing."

Chapter 4

I must be out of my mind, Lorren thought as she drove through the residential streets of Ennis toward Mama Nora's house. How could she have convinced herself to try and pull a fast one on Justin Madaris? Syneda was right. The man was no wimp. There was no doubt in Lorren's mind that he was way out of her league. But it was too late to back out of it now. She would have to go through with it and pray that somehow her plan worked.

What do I have to lose if it doesn't work? she asked herself as she pulled into Mama Nora's driveway. She dredged up a wavering smile. *Probably my peace of mind. Not to mention my sanity.*

* * *

"So..." Mama Nora poured herself a cup of coffee and sat at the table to join Lorren. "Have you finished unpacking?"

Lorren nodded. "Yes, except for the boxes that arrived this morning. I really appreciate your letting me use the lake house while I finish working on my book. The seclusion helps me concentrate."

"Mmmm." Mama Nora sipped the coffee she had poured into the cup. "And just how long will it take you to finish this book?"

"No more than two to three months at the most. Then I'll begin looking for a place to live somewhere in town before beginning a new book."

Mama Nora nodded. "I'm still not crazy about you being out there alone. But I feel a lot better, though, knowing Justin isn't far away."

Lorren leaned back in her chair. "You really like him, don't you?"

"Who? Justin? Sure I do. I've known the Madaris family for a long time. They're good people. Roman and Justin's daddy were roommates in college." Mama Nora took another sip of coffee before she continued. "Justin turned out to be a fine young man, even with all the pain he's suffered. He's worked hard over the years to mend that hole in his heart."

"Did you know his wife?"

"No, but I understand she was a sweet little thing, and that he simply adored her. It was sad how she died and so young." She shook her head. "I can remember his mama telling me how hard Justin had taken her death. For a while his family thought he'd never recover, that he had hardened his heart and would be a loner forever. But he pulled himself together and came around." Mama Nora swept a strand of gray hair over her left ear. "Yep, there's no doubt in my mind that one day he'll remarry."

Lorren refrained from making eye contact with Mama Nora. Instead, she fingered the pattern of the tablecloth. "Yes, he's said as much," she replied softly. "He certainly has an optimistic view on life. He claims he's waiting for fate to bring this special woman to him."

Mama Nora took another sip of coffee. "So I've heard. I hope it happens soon, and he gets just the kind of woman he needs. A good man like him shouldn't go to waste."

Lorren's head shot up. "Surely you don't believe in this fate stuff?"

"Me? Naw. But evidently Justin does, or at least he's convinced himself he does. People who have encountered pain in life will use just about anything as a safety net." She stared at Lorren. "You and Justin are alike in a way. Both of you are people made for love."

"Love? Me? Not hardly. I prefer just living, and to me living and loving don't necessarily go hand in hand. This business of love and marriage may be a turn-on for Justin, but they're a definite turnoff for me. I don't think I'll ever fully get over what Scott put me through…supposedly in the name of love."

Mama Nora touched Lorren's hand. "Believe this, child, all our hearts have been wounded in some kind of way. A person has to be able to dust herself off after a fall and move on. Somehow you got to get on with your life and not look back."

The words penetrated Lorren's mind. That was the whole idea of her moving back to Ennis—to get on with her life. And a man like Justin Madaris was too dangerous to the life she wanted. Whenever she was around him, she found herself thrown into one episode of blank-minded tizzies after another. He had the ability to stop her from thinking straight. She was determined more than ever to get him out of her life.

"Mmmm. Something smells delicious," Justin said, entering the house carrying a bottle of wine in one hand and a gym bag in the other.

Lorren's pulse quickened and her stomach fluttered nervously as she gazed up at him. Could she pull off what she'd planned? If so, before the evening was over she would scare the pants off him. Well…she really didn't want to go that far. The thought of Justin without pants was too much to think about. "It's gumbo. My roommate in college was from New Orleans and introduced me to Creole cooking. I hope you like it."

Justin broke into an open, friendly smile. "I'm sure I will."

Lorren couldn't help smiling back at him. Hurrying home from her visit with Mama Nora, she had dug through a box containing old magazines that had been delivered with her other stuff that morning. Rummaging through the box, she'd found an old magazine which contained the article, "Ways to Send an Overeager Male Running for Cover." She hoped the author of the article knew her stuff.

"Thanks for the wine, Justin. You can go on ahead. I'll join you after making sure everything's taken care of in the kitchen."

She tried not to give an overinterested glance at him. In swimming shorts, his physique was so well sculpted. Each muscle in his hard body was defined.

Justin pulled a towel out of the gym bag. "Oh yeah, will you go to the movies with me tomorrow night in Dallas?"

At any time she would have refused his invitation. But since chances were after tonight he would be avoiding her like the plague, she agreed to go for appearances' sake. "Sure, I'd love to."

Justin gave her a smile that sent her pulse racing. "Great!"

Lorren took a deep breath when Justin left. *Get your act together, girl, and don't screw up.*

When she reached the lake Justin was already in the water. The only part of him visible was his naked brown chest. She slowly disrobed, revealing her two-piece swimming suit, fully aware his eyes were on her.

Calling out to him, she asked, "How cold is the water?"

"It's not cold at all, which is surprising for a day in April," he answered, taking in every detail of the exotic orchid print bathing suit that was molded to all her curves. "Come on in," he invited.

Lorren couldn't help noticing the interest he was showing in her outfit.

"You look absolutely sensational, Lorren."

She smiled. "Thanks." She then dived down deep into the water, resurfacing seconds later. She pushed the wet hair from her eyes. "Justin Madaris! I thought you said the water wasn't cold! It's freezing in here!"

Justin laughed a throaty laugh. "No, it's not," he said, swimming toward her. "Just relax. You'll get used to the temperature."

"I—I doubt it," she muttered in a chattering voice.

"Oh, come here, you big baby, let me warm you." Before she could react, he was wrapping his arms around her. "Does that feel better?"

Lorren nodded, unable to speak. His arms were holding her gently. The motion of the water nudged them together from breast to thigh. She was aware of Justin's solidly built body. The water pushed them even closer, and her breasts brushed against his chest. The muscles of her abdomen quivered.

Justin felt Lorren's breasts swell against him. He ached to remove her top and rub his thumb against their taut tips. How many times had he fantasized about holding her like this, so achingly close to his aroused body? Even now, he could smell her perfume, an alluring scent that made him want to...

Suddenly, with trembling hands, he released her. He had to resist temptation. "That should warm you up some," he murmured huskily. "Come on. Let's swim for a while."

Lorren nodded. His touch hadn't just warmed her; it nearly had her in flames.

They swam, hard and fast, their arms splashing vigorously through the water, trying to channel their powerful heat for one another into playful activities. For an entire hour they had a gung ho time treading water and engaging in water wars. Twice when he caught her trying to cheat during a race, he grabbed her and pulled her under. Once, after making it to the other side and resting on the edge, he jumped out of the water and tossed her up in the air and out over the water.

"Justin Madaris! You're going to pay dearly for doing that!" she screamed.

He threw his head back, releasing a great peal of laughter before diving in. Coming up beside her, his arms wrapped around her waist. "Threats!" he teased.

In spite of herself, Lorren joined him in laughter. They trod water some more before swimming to the other side again.

"If we don't get out of here soon, we'll start looking like prunes," she said. "Besides, it's almost dinnertime."

Justin gave her a devastating smile. "My stomach agrees with you." He got out of the water. "I really enjoyed myself, Lorren. You're a lot of fun."

"I had a great time, too," she replied, getting out of the water and toweling herself. *Too great a time,* she thought, grabbing her robe. A feeling of happiness rose inside her, making her feel lighthearted and relaxed. This was the most fun she'd had with a man in a long time.

"Allow me." Justin took the robe from her fingers and held it out so she could slip her arms into the sleeves. His hands smoothed the fabric around her shoulders, down her back, and over the curve of her hips. He was tempted to go farther, to run his hands lightly up the insides of her thighs, to make her ache for him as much as he was aching for her.

Lorren's head was whirling. How could his touch have this effect on her? His arms were now around her waist, forcing her against his body so she could not ignore his want of her. She closed her eyes. She couldn't give in. "Thanks, Justin," she whispered.

"You're welcome." His hot breath caressed her ear. "Are you ready?"

His husky voice reverberated through her body. "Ready?"

Justin turned her around to face him. His hand moved caressingly along her side. "Yeah. Are you ready to go?"

Unable to speak at the moment, Lorren nodded.

They walked back to the lake house. Justin drew her closer to his side, making her aware of the strength radiating from him as well as the power of his body. When they entered the house, she attempted to breathe normally. It wasn't easy. His proximity had nearly stolen the air from her lungs.

"Is the spare bedroom okay?" Justin asked.

His question startled her. "For what?"

"To change clothes."

"Oh. Sure," she replied, embarrassed that she'd jumped to conclusions. "I'll meet you back here in a few minutes."

They returned to the living room about the same time. Lorren had changed into a pair of shorts and a T-shirt, and Justin was wearing jeans and a sweatshirt. She noticed the gold coin medallion around his neck. "That's a nice medallion, Justin."

"Thanks," he replied, unconsciously tucking it inside his sweatshirt. "Do you need help preparing anything?" he asked.

"No thanks. Just make yourself comfortable. It'll only take a few minutes to warm up everything," she replied, rushing off to the kitchen. The man was too sexy for words.

Back in the kitchen, she busied herself with dinner, trying not to think about the man in the other room. The gumbo's spicy aroma helped clear her mind.

In the living room, Justin glanced up at a huge painting Lorren had hanging on the wall. It was a painting of two African children, a boy and a girl. Both were dressed in their native apparel. "Who are they?" Justin asked, turning in Lorren's direction and asking the question across the open breakfast bar separating the kitchen from the living room.

Lorren glanced up and saw him standing in front of the painting. She smiled at him. "Evidently you've never read any of my Kente Kids books, Justin," she said teasingly. "Or you would know that's Suma and Zakiya, my two original Kente Kids. They are everybody's favorites. Suma is a male African name which means the first one, and Zakiya is a female African name which means smart and intelligent. Every so often, I introduce a new Kente Kid in one of my books. That's what I'm doing in the book I'm presently working on. There are now a total of six Kente Kids."

"And who's the new kid?" Justin asked, grinning.

"A little boy by the name of Mukasas. His name means giver and provider."

"That's interesting." He turned his head back to the painting. "I wouldn't mind having a copy of this painting for my very own."

Lorren grinned. Like Justin, most people were immediately taken with her Kente Kids. "Sorry, that painting is one of a kind. It was painted by a friend of mine from college and given to me as a gift."

Justin nodded as he glanced around the room. He noticed a stack of boxes sitting on the floor in the corner. "You're still unpacking?"

"Yes. Those boxes arrived this morning. I'm not sure whether or not I'll be unpacking all of that stuff. Other than the items I need for my writing, I'm going to wait until I'm settled into my own place before unpacking most of it."

"Will you be moving into town?"

"Yes, but I'm in no hurry. I like the privacy and the seclusion this place provides. I wish I could talk Mama Nora into selling it to me. It's just what I need. I don't want anything too big. It's perfect."

Justin walked into the kitchen as Lorren was making the salad. "Why don't you ask her?"

She shook her head. "I can't do that. She loves this place as much as I do."

Justin nodded. "How would you like leasing the one I'm in?"

Lorren looked startled. "Where're you going?"

Justin's mouth curved into a smile. "I'm buying the Taylors' place. In fact, I'm meeting with the attorneys tomorrow to sign the final papers. That's the reason for the cookout on Thursday. It's sort of a celebration. I've been negotiating with the seller for over four months now. We've finally reached a satisfactory agreement."

"You bought Taylor Oaks?" she asked, totally surprised. In her early days in Ennis, Taylor Oaks had been one of the largest spreads in the county. Sam and Holly Taylor had been members of Ennis's elite society. Their beautiful cattle ranch had also been the sight for breeding thoroughbred horses. It was situated on over three hundred acres of land encompassing the most beautiful oak trees found anywhere. That ranch had been Lorren's dream home since the time she'd first attended the Taylors' annual barbecue. She used to envision herself living there.

Mama Nora had informed her last year of the

Taylors' deaths when their private plane had crashed. Because they left no children, the ranch became the property of a wealthy distant relative. Uninterested in the ranch, he had put it up for sale.

"Yes, I bought Taylor Oaks." Justin leaned proudly against the kitchen door. "It cost me a bundle, but I think it's a worthwhile investment. I knew I wanted it the moment I saw it."

"But it's so huge. Isn't it too big for one person?"

Justin smiled. "I plan on closing my office in town and moving it to the ranch. I'm converting a section of the house downstairs into an office and examining rooms. And I do plan on remarrying one day and want a large family, so the size of it will fit perfectly with my future plans."

"When will you be moving?"

"Not for a while. I'm going to have the place completely renovated. It's been empty for over a year."

"That's wonderful, Justin. Congratulations."

"Thanks. Are you sure you don't need any help?"

Lorren smiled. "Positive. Everything's all set."

During dinner Justin told her some more about his family and his childhood escapades.

"My goodness," she said, filled with laughter. "You and your siblings were definitely a rowdy bunch. It's a wonder your parents didn't snip your ears."

Justin laughed. "Believe me, there were moments when they were tempted. My two brothers and I used to fight like hell among ourselves, but when it came to protecting each other against some outsider who tried to bother any one of us, we stuck together like glue."

Lorren smiled. "Where's your family now?"

"In Houston. Both of my parents are college professors at Texas Southern. My youngest sister, Christy, will be sixteen next month. She claims being the youngest in the family isn't much fun with three overprotective older brothers. My other sisters, Kattie and Traci, are both married. Neither of my brothers is married. Dex is only eighteen months younger than me. He was married for a short while, but things didn't work out. He works for a major oil company in Australia. We're expecting him back in the States any day, and I'm looking forward to it. I haven't seen him in almost two years. My brother Clayton is three years younger than me, and is an attorney in Houston. He's flying in for the cookout, so you'll get to meet him then."

Lorren's eyes sparkled with admiration for the obvious warmth and affection Justin felt for his family. "Any nieces or nephews?"

Justin grinned. "Not enough according to my parents. Kattie and Traci both have two kids each, all boys. My parents are anxiously awaiting their first granddaughter. Since Kattie and Traci claim they're not having any more kids, my parents aren't too pleased with the marital status of me and my brothers."

Lorren smiled as Justin finished off the last of the gumbo soup she'd served with a tossed salad. She removed their dishes from the table to the sink. "Go on into the living room. I'll bring dessert right out."

She came into the living room a few minutes

later, carrying a tray with cut slices of apple pie which she placed on the coffee table.

A big smile covered Justin's face as he tasted the pie. "This is delicious. Is it homemade?"

Lorren grinned. "Thanks, and yes, I made it myself. Everyone who lived with Mama Nora left with a degree in baking."

A while later Lorren gathered their dishes and took them into the kitchen. When she returned she switched on the tape player sitting on a nearby table. The soft melodic sound of Luther Vandross filled the air.

"Dinner was great, Lorren."

"Thanks."

"Come here." Justin's voice was husky as he patted the spot next to him on the sofa.

As much as she hated doing so, especially when she was enjoying his company, the time had come to send Justin running for cover. Taking a deep breath, she joined him on the sofa. "Would you care for some more wine, Justin?"

"No, this is fine." He spread his arms out along the back of the sofa, then slipped his hand to the nape of Lorren's neck.

She turned toward him slightly, clearing her throat. "Did you have a busy day?"

He rubbed his finger against her cheek. "No busier than most."

"Oh," she replied as she watched him drink his wine, thinking how sensuous his mouth was. She couldn't help remembering the feel of that mouth on hers. How he had run his tongue over her lips.

How his tongue had parted her mouth and slipped inside to...*Good grief! What's wrong with me?* she shifted frantically in her seat. She felt Justin's hand move from her cheek to her shoulder. His fingers traced a heated path down her arm.

Lorren bolted from her seat.

"Justin, there's something I'd like to give you."

Confusion appeared on Justin's face when he watched her lift the sofa pillow she'd been sitting on and pull out an envelope, dropping the pillow back in place.

"Here."

Justin eyed the envelope she held out to him. His gaze returned to her, bewilderment evident in his features. "What is it?"

"Read it and see."

Justin stood and, taking the envelope from Lorren's hand, opened it. A legal-looking document was inside. He pulled it out and glanced at it, then looked back at her. "A preaffair agreement?"

"Yes, it's the latest thing. Isn't that neat? It spells out all my requirements."

"What requirements?"

"The requirements you have to agree to before I'd consider having an affair with you."

Justin stared at her in disbelief, then back at the paper he held in his hand. A shudder slithered down his spine. How could he have been so wrong about her? Not in a million years would he have thought there was a conniving bone in her body. Had this evening been nothing but a setup?

A part of his mind sent him an entirely different message. His expression suddenly turned thoughtful as his gaze moved over Lorren's features. She glanced nervously around the room, refusing to look at him. Justin backtracked his thoughts to earlier that evening. Memories tugged at him—their swim and how much fun they'd had, the expression on her face when he'd told her about his family, how she'd listened and the smile she'd worn. A part of him simply refused to believe this entire evening had meant absolutely nothing to her but a ploy to put him on a leash. Still, the piece of paper in his hand proved otherwise.

What were these requirements Lorren wanted? And did she really expect him to go along with them? He doubted it, which meant she knew he wouldn't. Was that what she was counting on? There was only one way to find out. He glanced down and briefly read the typewritten, legal-looking document. A few minutes later he glanced up at her, shaking his head. "Is this a joke?"

To Lorren's surprise, Justin sounded amused, not angered. "No."

"Your first requirement is unlimited use of my Vette?"

Lorren raised her chin. "That's right. Hopefully, I won't need to use it often, but I want to know if I ever needed to, there wouldn't be a problem. I detest a man who thinks more of a piece of tin than he does the woman in his life."

She saw a flash of disbelief cross Justin's face. "My Vette is not a piece of tin, Lorren. Can you handle a Vette?"

Lorren lifted a dark brow. "Justin, we're talking about a car, not a spaceship. What's there to handle? If you've driven one automobile, you've driven them all. I could never understand why some men think car manufacturers make certain vehicles just for them. There's not a car on the road that a woman can't handle."

Justin shook his head. He didn't have the time to disagree with her. He looked back down at the paper. Moments later his head shot up. "Your second requirement is that your name be added to my checking account?" he asked incredulously.

Lorren smiled. "Yeah. I thought that was a great idea. You wouldn't believe just how stingy some men are. Any man I become involved with will have to make sure I never run out of money. I'm sure being a doctor pays well, so you won't have a thing to worry about. Any money you make will be our money."

When Justin spoke his tone was dry. "No kidding? And what about the money you make?"

Lorren chuckled. "Any money I make will be *my* money, of course."

"Of course. How foolish of me to think otherwise."

"What do you think of my final requirement? Of course it's nothing you can do right away, but as long as you'll agree to it, that will be fine." Lorren took a deep breath. This one was a doozy.

"Let me make sure I understand this correctly," Justin said moments later, his voice low and dangerously controlled. "You want a child...out of wedlock?"

"Yes. As I've told you before, I've no intentions of remarrying, but I do want to have a child before I'm thirty. I'll have full custody; all you have to do is provide me with generous child support payments."

Justin looked at her intently. "You aren't serious about these requirements, are you?"

"Yes. I'm dead serious."

"And you won't agree to an affair until I've agreed to them?"

"That's the bottom line, Justin."

Lorren smiled sweetly. She could just imagine the thoughts tumbling through his mind. Her requirements were ludicrous. He would never agree to any of them. No man would. According to the magazine article, not too many men willingly turn over their prized autos to a woman. Very few of them parted easily with their hard-earned dollars, and what man wanted to pay through the nose for child support payments? Being caught in that sort of a trap was something they tried to avoid.

Justin watched a satisfied smile quirk the corners of Lorren's lips. She was having her laugh, or so she thought. Now he would have his.

"Well, there's nothing else for me to do, Lorren."

Lorren's smile widened. She watched as he fished in his pocket for his keys.

Her brow arched in confusion. He hadn't driven over, he'd walked. What on earth did he need his keys for? As she continued watching, he took a key off the ring and placed it on the table.

"That's the key to the Vette. I'll use the spare I have at home."

Lorren stared at him with openmouthed shock, totally speechless. She then watched him reach into his back pocket and pull out a checkbook that looked like it had seen better days.

"I'll add your name to my account first thing in the morning, as soon as the bank opens. You can use these until new checks arrive."

When in one swift motion he stripped his sweat-shirt off over his head, Lorren found her voice. "What are you doing?"

Justin looked at her. A huge grin touched his mouth. "Getting ready to give you that baby you want before you're thirty. I know you have a few years left before then, but practice makes perfect, you know." He almost laughed out loud at her look of amazement.

Lorren's heart jumped in her chest. What had she gotten herself into? Justin, bare-chested except for the medallion around his neck, and a sexy smile, took a step toward her.

She took a step back, rubbing her hands together. "It—it was a joke," she managed to get out.

Justin smiled, taking another step forward, covering the distance between them. "What was a joke?" he asked in a deep, sexy voice. He stood before her appearing completely relaxed.

Lorren cleared her throat. "I got this stupid idea and it was supposed to work." Justin didn't comment, which struck Lorren as strange. He just continued looking at her. "You weren't supposed to agree to my requirements," she continued.

She tried not to focus her attention on his shoulders. They were broad and powerful. She suspected those shoulders would feel massive against the palms of her hands. She drew a very slow, very deep breath, trying to put a halt to where her thoughts were headed, praying they hadn't shown on her face.

"And just what was I supposed to do, Lorren?"

She tried to ignore the fluttering in her stomach produced by the deep, husky sound of his voice. She had gotten herself in enough trouble. "You were supposed to be scared off."

Justin's shoulders moved in a dismissive gesture. "I don't scare easily." He took another step forward, bringing him directly in front of her.

Lorren's eyes fastened on the play of rippling muscles across his chest. Heat flared in the pit of her stomach. The look in his eyes was dangerous. The air surrounding them seemed to thicken. She lifted her chin. "I can see that."

"But what I do, Lorren, is get even."

She swallowed hard. "Get even? How?"

"A number of ways. But this way is just for you." He leaned forward, his breath misted across her mouth. The touch of Justin's lips was gentle. His tongue playfully massaged her lips, seeking entry.

"Open your mouth to me, Lorren."

The plea whispered softly against her lips had a hypnotic effect, and, taking a deep, unsteady breath, her mouth formed the word "no," but instead she did as he requested. His tender caresses destroyed her last thread of resistance. She surrendered completely to his masterful seduction and placed her arms around him.

His mouth, wet and hot, nibbled at hers with a hunger that was mind consuming. The burning sensation flooding through her was unbearable.

The kiss grew hotter, hungrier.

Lorren could feel every hard-muscled inch of Justin, including evidence of his desire for her. A powerful tremor swept through her body as she fought for control. The little bit she had took a nosedive when she felt his hand move underneath her top. She shuddered involuntarily at the multitude of emotions overwhelming her with his touch. Deep in the recesses of her mind she wanted to put a stop to what they were doing, but couldn't find the strength to do so.

When his arms tightened around her, prolonging the kiss, she melted into him. An indescribable sweetness flared in her belly, stripping away the last of her defenses. Releasing a soft moan, her tongue met his, stroke for stroke.

Without any control she slid her hands between

them to rub his chest. The feel of his chest hair against her palms made her entire body tingle. Her hands brushed against the medallion. His body instantly stiffened. He pulled his mouth away.

Lorren was breathless. Confused. Why had he stopped kissing her? Before she had time to think about it, he leaned down to brush his lips against her cheek. Then his mouth was on hers again and all thoughts flooded from her mind.

Capturing her hands, he pulled them around him, coaxing her arms to wrap around his waist as she pulled herself closer to him.

Their kiss intensified. She could feel the pressure of his other hand in the curve of her back, drawing her closer to him, urging her more intimately into the fit of him. For the first time in her life, she knew how it felt to become insane with the need of someone.

Justin released her mouth. His voice was thick with desire. "Baby, let's finish this in the bedroom."

His words intruded like a blast of cold air, snapping Lorren back to reality. She jerked away from him and began straightening her clothes. She struggled to hide her confusion over what she'd felt—an upsurge of devouring yearning. It was an emotion too new to her. Disconcerted, she crossed her arms and pointedly looked away from him. What had gotten into her? Why had she let him kiss her like that, knowing nothing would come of it? Why on earth did she enjoy his kisses so much?

Out of the corner of her eye she saw Justin

fighting for control. His breathing was deep and rapid. He would want answers, but she wouldn't give him any. She couldn't.

"Lorren?"

Unlike earlier, he said her name in a voice with a cutting edge to it. If he was upset with her, that was too friggin' bad. She could deal better with his anger than his disappointment. Never again would she see the look of total sexual letdown on the face of another man.

Still she couldn't bring herself to look at him. How could she face him?

"Lorren, look at me!"

She flinched at the hardness of his command. No matter what, she wouldn't look at him. "Please leave, Justin. Tonight was a mistake."

Justin frowned. There was something about the tone of her words that cooled his anger. Her voice sounded tired and laced with hopelessness.

With a sense of purpose he didn't understand, he walked over to her and took her into his arms. She tried pulling away, but he wouldn't let her. She still refused to look at him. "What's wrong, Lorren?"

"Nothing's wrong. And no matter what you think, especially after tonight, I'm not easy, Justin." The words were spoken barely above a whisper.

Justin lifted her chin, forcing her eyes to meet his. The depth of pain he saw confused him. The pallidness of her nutmeg skin disturbed him. He touched a finger gently to her swollen lips, sealing off any further words of protest. "I don't think you're easy, Lorren. In fact, I think you're complicated as hell."

Lorren pulled away from him.

This time Justin let her.

"Please leave, Justin. I want to be alone."

He hesitated before speaking. "All right. If that's what you want. I need to get my bag out of the spare bedroom."

Minutes later he returned to find her standing by the door as if anxious for his departure. "Are you sure you're okay, Lorren?"

She nodded. "You can have these back," she said, handing him the key and his sweatshirt and checkbook, being careful not to touch him. "As I said, Justin, I did it as a joke."

Justin reached out and took her hand. She tried pulling away, but he held on to her wrist. Their gazes held as his hand slipped from her wrist, and he threaded his fingers through hers. "Someone once told me years ago that no matter how painful your yesterdays were, there's always tomorrow. I'm passing that same message on to you. Think about it."

With those final words, he released her hand, squeezing it gently before letting go. Turning, he walked out into the warm Texas night.

Chapter 5

Moonlight sliced a thick silver path across the water, bathing the lush grasslands in a magical glow.

Emerging naked from the waters of the lake, Justin shivered in the cool, damp air. With a grimace, he pulled on his pants over his wet skin.

Gathering up the rest of his clothing, he started walking back to his house. He glanced toward the house where Lorren was probably sleeping and slowed his steps. His eyes didn't blink for the longest time as he stared at the outline of the structure through the trees.

He stopped walking as thoughts of Lorren consumed his mind. There was no mistaking the woman had a problem. And it was deep enough to drive her to the point of pulling a stunt like the one she'd pulled tonight. What exactly had her ex-husband done to make her feel the need to protect herself so fiercely? What had he done to put that tone of hopelessness in her voice, that look of sadness in her eyes? He wondered if she'd ever really experienced a loving relationship at any point during her marriage.

The enormity of those questions propelled him forward toward his place, wondering where he could find some answers. Would Ms. Nora tell him if he asked? What about her friend, Syneda?

Unlocking his door he stepped inside, allowing his eyes to adjust to the room's darkness. He closed the door behind him, then leaned against it. What was there about Lorren that made him even care enough to want to know?

That's an easy question, man, his mind replied. *The woman's kisses have only whet your appetite. Her resistance has only increased your determination. And surprisingly, though it seems otherwise, it's not all about sex. She's the first woman who's actually gotten next to you, really next to you, since Denise.*

Justin was grateful the door supported his back as the realization hit him full force. He ran a hand over his unshaven chin. The last thing he needed in his life was any complications.

He laughed. *Think again, bro. Lorren Jacobs is clearly a complication.*

There was a lot about her he didn't know, a lot he didn't understand. But then there was something he did know, and that was that whatever problems she'd had in the past, the last thing she needed was a man who'd allow her to wallow in self-pity; a man who'd easily give up on her and her cynical facade. What she needed was someone willing to explore the woman hidden underneath her hard shell—no matter what roadblocks she tried putting in his way. She needed a man capable of giving her tender, loving care.

Point-blank, she needed him.

Everyone was entitled to experience a loving relationship at least once in a lifetime. Even one with no strings attached. As far as he was concerned, Lorren's time had come.

After a sleepless night, Lorren got out of bed early to start writing. She hoped it would erase Justin from her mind. How could she have been so stupid to think she could stand a chance against him?

Hours later she sat at her personal computer in deep concentration, keying her thoughts into it. She was having fun writing about Mukasas, her newest Kente Kid. Her agent was presently negotiating a deal with a major toy manufacturer, who was interested in transforming her ethnic book characters into cute, cuddly, and culturally rich toys. Lorren felt very excited about the project that would introduce her "kids" into even more households. She was so involved in working on her story that the ringing of the telephone startled her.

"Yes?"

"Good morning."

The husky, sensuous sound of Justin Madaris's voice filtered through the telephone lines. Lorren's stomach twisted in knots. Had he called to gloat about last night?

"What do you want, Justin?"

Justin clenched his hands into fists inside his pockets. He wondered if her mouth was swollen from his kisses of last night. Thinking about it made his blood race. He took a deep steadying breath. "Tsk, Ms. Jacobs. You were a lot more neighborly yesterday."

Lorren glanced at the computer monitor before her. The characters seemed to darken before her eyes. She knew it wasn't the monitor, but her mood. "So I'm fickle. Sue me."

"I'd rather make love to you," Justin replied, his voice low, deep, and sexy.

Lorren was glad she was sitting down. Sensational shivers streaked through her body. She'd recognized desire in his eyes before, but until now, he'd only hinted at wanting her. She had never expected him to actually say the words, and his doing so now had her gasping for air. "Don't say that," she whispered through jagged breaths, her words soft.

"Why not? It's the truth, and we both know it.

Don't you think it's time we began being honest with each other?"

Lorren closed her eyes, trying not to conjure up visions of them last night, wrapped in each other's arms, kissing. He'd desired her last night—she might be a novice in some things, but that much she was sure of. However, would his desire have slowed to a fizzle once he'd gotten her in the bedroom? She didn't know and wouldn't give herself a chance to find out.

"Why're you calling, Justin?" she asked curtly. "Don't you have patients to see, examinations to perform, sinusitis or arthritis to cure?"

"The reason I'm calling is to find out what time you want me to pick you up tonight."

Lorren's brow lifted. "Pick me up? For what?"

"The movies. Have you forgotten our date?"

Lorren groaned inwardly. She'd only agreed to go out with him because she thought her plans to get him out of her life were a sure thing.

"And don't try getting out of it, Lorren. You said you'd go with me, and I took you at your word. Besides, if nothing else, you have to admit we do enjoy each other's company."

Lorren sighed. His words held the truth. She'd had more fun with him yesterday than she'd had in a long time. Her ability to laugh seemed to blossom around him. And if she was completely honest with herself, she'd have to admit she couldn't really blame him for the fact she had made a complete fool of herself with the stunt she'd pulled.

She stared pensively into space. She hadn't been to a movie in years, which in itself was unusual for someone who lived in Los Angeles. Besides, one thing Mama Nora had always taught them was to face any problems head-on, no matter how big or small. And with Scott, she'd done just the opposite. Now she was making the same mistake with Justin. Instead of standing up to him, she'd been retreating.

It was obvious he had no intentions of leaving her alone, and she refused to spend the rest of her days living in Ennis avoiding him. He was a problem she would have to deal with directly. Pretty soon he would tire of pursuing her. Then, like all the others, he'd leave her alone and move on to some other viable conquest.

"How about it, Lorren? Are you still going?"

Silence hung in the air. "Yes, I'm still going."

"Is seven o'clock okay?"

Lorren took a deep breath. "Yes, seven o'clock is fine. I'll be ready."

"Why are we here, Justin?"

"I thought it was a lovely night to park awhile. Don't you like the view?"

"I'd rather go home." Lorren sighed. Up to now the evening had gone the way she had hoped. Justin had arrived at precisely seven, dressed in a pair of snug-fitting jeans and a white cotton shirt. And, as usual, he looked devastatingly sexy.

She'd worn a denim wrap skirt and a loose white

pullover shirt. A pair of flat slingbacks adorned her feet. A necklace of graduated bone-colored wooden disks graced her neck with coordinating earrings for her ears. Justin had taken one look at her and his mouth had fallen open. The expression on his chestnut face had been purely comical.

"Well, Justin. Are we going to the movies or are we going to miss most of it while you stand there gawking?"

The movie had been a comedy, and they had shared laughter the entire time. After the movie they'd gone to a café in the West End Market Place for coffee. On the way home he had taken a sharp turn off the highway, heading toward Bristol Trail, a wooded area reputed to be a nighttime hideaway for lovers.

Lorren's mind returned to the present as Justin shifted positions in the car seat. He turned to her and openly studied both her and the outfit she wore. His eyes boldly scanned her from head to toe. She tensed under his close examination, suddenly feeling underdressed. His gaze locked with hers, as if trying to penetrate every defense she had. And to her dismay, it was beginning to work.

"Take me home, Justin. We're a bit too old for this sort of thing."

A slow smile tilted Justin's lips. "You're never too old for lovers' lane."

Lorren shook her head, more than slightly annoyed. "That's your opinion. I happen to disagree."

"Did you enjoy the movie?"

"Yes. Thanks for taking me. Now take me home."

"I brought you here to ask a favor of you."

She raised a suspicious brow. "What kind of favor?"

"How would you like to go camping with me this weekend?"

"No, I *don't* think so."

Justin smiled. "Relax. We won't be alone. In fact, you'll be the only female with me and five other guys."

Lorren's eyes widened. "You can't be serious!"

Seeing the look of shock on her face, Justin laughed. "On the contrary, I'm completely serious. But before you get all bent out of shape, I'll level with you. The other guys are between the ages of five and ten."

Lorren frowned, her eyes puzzled. "I don't understand."

"I'm a volunteer at the Children's Home Society. A group of the little guys and I are going camping this weekend. The Society has a policy that there has to be at least two adults for every five kids. My usual partner can't make it, so I'm asking you to fill in as his replacement."

"And I'll be the only female?"

"Yeah, for my group. Friends of mine from Dallas—John and his wife, Juanita—will be camping in the site next to us with another group."

"What happens if you can't find a replacement?"

"Then I won't have any other choice but to cancel

the trip. And I'd hate to do that. The boys have been looking forward to this outing for quite a while."

Lorren sighed. Should she consider going? She would hate for the little guys to be disappointed if the trip had to be canceled. Growing up in a foster home, she knew how important outings were.

"Are you sure there's no one else you can ask?"

"Yeah, I'm sure. There's no one else I can ask at this late date."

"Will the boys have any qualms about a woman tagging along?"

"Erick will probably have something to say at first, but he'll get over it. He still classifies girls in the same category as spinach. Yucky, yuck."

A smile touched Lorren's lips. "What you're doing with the boys is real special, Justin. One of the things I appreciated most when I lived with Mama Nora was the people who unselfishly gave their time to us."

Justin noticed how her face became even more beautiful when she was pleased with something. "Then you'll go?"

"Yeah. I'll go."

"Great. My parents' friends from Dallas let me borrow their recreational vehicle whenever I take the boys camping. I'm picking it up late Friday afternoon. We'll leave around six o'clock Saturday morning."

Lorren nodded, a smile pursing her lips. "You didn't have to bring me to Bristol Trail to ask me about the camping trip."

She glanced toward the rear of the car. "I guess I should be glad your Vette doesn't have a back seat. I wouldn't want you to get any ideas," she said, grinning, beginning to feel relaxed.

There was teasing laughter in Justin's eyes. "Shame on you. You're behind the times. No one uses a back seat anymore."

Lorren tried suppressing a giggle. "No? What're they using now?"

"The hood."

Lorren couldn't help herself as she burst out laughing at Justin's reply. Justin found himself joining her infectious laughter.

Suddenly, their amusement died simultaneously. All traces of humor were replaced by raw desire. Their gazes held. Their breathing quickened in unison. Concurrent shivers surged through their veins.

Justin slowly leaned forward, his eyes focused on Lorren's mouth. She felt paralyzed under his intense gaze. Her pulse became erratic.

He touched her forearm. The heat of the caress made Lorren feel dizzy. Warmth radiated in her throat. Liquid heat raced from her head to her toes—and he hadn't even kissed her yet.

Her breath sharpened painfully as his mouth came closer; the manly scent of his cologne was overwhelming. A soft groan escaped her throat. Her mouth burned with anticipation. Desire bubbled within her like a geyser, filling her with a strange inner excitement.

Justin flicked his tongue over her bottom lip, making her shiver. His tongue leisurely outlined her upper lip. She melted. Lorren felt the thrusting pressure as his tongue entered her mouth. She died a slow, erotic death as their mouths mated, hotly, hungrily.

He pulled her across the seat and into his lap, cradling her intimately, crushing her breasts against his chest. He kissed her with searing intensity, with heated longing, with unconcealed wanting. The kiss was greedy, sensuous, deep. His hands moved in provocative caresses over her back and down her legs.

Lorren clung to him, as a hot glowing ache began radiating from the very core of her. Sinking even deeper into his arms, her body responded to his seduction, slow and hot.

A loud crash jarred them from the heated moment, and they parted quickly.

"What the…"

"What was that?" Lorren's voice was slurred with passion, her lips wet from his kiss. She moved from Justin's lap and back into her seat, straightening her clothing.

Justin shook his head, his breathing coming in short gasps. "I don't know, but I intend to find out. It sounded like an accident or something."

Backing his car out of the secluded spot, he headed toward the highway. They hadn't driven far when they spotted an overturned vehicle on the road. Reacting with undaunting speed, Justin used his cellular phone to call for help. Then, grabbing his medical bag from the back of the car, he ran toward the vehicle. Chills swept over Lorren's body as she followed him to offer her assistance.

"Go back, Lorren," he ordered, taking immediate charge of the situation. "This car might blow any minute. There're two people inside. I have to get to them and check the extent of their injuries. Call 911 again and tell them to get a chopper in here fast. It looks pretty bad, and I can't risk moving them."

Lorren did as Justin instructed, moving swiftly. When she returned moments later, he had crawled through a broken window and was inside the car, administering medical aid to the victims. She noticed they were teenagers, a girl and a boy.

Standing a safe distance away, she watched Justin. Gone was the taunting gleam in his eyes and the suggestive smile tilting his lips. Both had been replaced by frowns of deep concern and compassion. She fought back the bile threatening to rise in her throat at the sight of the teenagers' physical condition. She felt faint. "Justin, are they—"

"They're alive, Lorren, but barely. I hope the chopper gets here soon. They need to be transported to the hospital immediately. Both have extensive injuries."

A few minutes later the sound of a chopper could be heard overhead and the loud squeal of sirens followed. Shortly thereafter, the area was swarming with help.

Justin beckoned to her when both victims were being loaded in the chopper. "I'm going with them to the hospital. It was touch and go there for a while with the girl, so say a prayer for both of them. Drive the Vette back to your place. I don't know how long I'll be, so just leave the keys under your mat."

"How will you get home?"

"I'll get one of the officers to drop me off." He quickly brushed her lips with his. Then, turning, he ran toward the chopper.

Lorren got in Justin's car. Before starting the ignition she bent her head and said a prayer.

Lorren threw off the bedcovers when she heard the sound of a car pulling into the driveway. Not bothering to slip into her robe, she quickly went into the kitchen and turned on the coffeemaker. A quick glance at the kitchen clock indicated it was almost three o'clock.

Peeping out the window, she saw Justin get out of a patrol car. He headed toward the porch to retrieve his keys from under the mat. She opened the door. "Justin?"

Justin came toward her, then stopped. Hooking his thumbs in the waistband of his jeans, he cocked his head to one side. "What are you doing up?"

"I couldn't sleep." She moved aside, holding the door open for him. "Come in. I've made coffee."

Inside, in full view of the lights, she saw lines of strain and fatigue etched on his face. Without further thought, she took his hand and led him into the kitchen. She poured a steaming cup of coffee and gave it to him.

Justin gazed into the dark murky substance before lifting the brew to his lips. He raised his head and met her eyes, knowing the questions lodged there. "They're in critical condition. Let's pray they make it."

He let out a deep breath, and his eyes bored into Lorren. "They had a high alcohol level, way over the limits. Can you believe that? The boy is only seventeen and the girl is sixteen. And to top if off, neither of them were wearing seat belts. It's a wonder they weren't killed instantly. If we hadn't heard the crash, there's no telling what would've happened. That stretch of highway is pretty much deserted after midnight."

His voice crumbled slightly. "They're just kids, Lorren. Kids who should have a full life ahead of them, going swimming, skating, dancing. Kids who should not have been drinking. The girl is just a few months older than my baby sister."

Instinctively, Lorren put her arm around Justin and pressed her head against his chest. He was a man who had dedicated his life to helping others, but he was also human. And at the moment, the human side of him agonized over a senseless accident. His hold on her tightened, and she knew he was trying to come to grips with what he'd witnessed tonight.

She pulled back and gave him a quick kiss on the cheek. "You did all you could, Justin. And you may have saved their lives. You even risked your own life by getting inside that car to help them. The car could have caught fire at any moment. I was so proud of you tonight."

Justin slipped an arm around Lorren and drew her back against the hard warmth of his chest. She became confused with the feelings of warmth and protectiveness he was stirring in her. The thought that she could protect him from anything was absolutely ridiculous. But still, she couldn't help feeling she was comforting him in some way.

Lorren intended to place another kiss on his cheek, but he turned and caught her lips with his. Her mouth responded to the gentle probing of his tongue. He drew her closer to him. She moved her hips and gasped when she felt his hardness pressed against her.

Justin gently caressed her mouth with slow moist strokes, building pleasure inside of her with each second that ticked by. He thoroughly explored the insides of her lips, drawing one into his mouth, sucking on it. She groaned at the sensations churning inside her.

"Let me love you, Lorren. Please." His plea, spoken huskily in her ear, sent shivers down her body. He hadn't demanded anything from her with dirty words, as Scott had always done. His words were soft and sensual. And he wasn't handling her roughly either. He was touching her as though she were a fine piece of china. She shivered as his caresses became more sensual, more heated through the fabric of her nightgown. Her breathing quickened along with his. She knew where they were headed if she didn't stop him. But for the life of her, she couldn't.

And deep down, she didn't want to.

Please let all of Scott's accusations be lies. Please don't let me disappoint Justin. More than anything else in the world, tonight I want Scott to be wrong about me. Please let it be so. Please.

"Please." Her lips whispered the words in his mouth. Slipping her arms around his neck, she melted into his embrace. "Please."

Justin's eyes smoldered with desire when he raised his head. In one smooth movement he swept Lorren into his arms. She closed her eyes and brushed her face against his throat as he carried her from the kitchen to the bedroom. Once there he gently placed her on the bed in the tangle of bedcovers, then joined her, pulling her into his arms.

His lips again took hers, his tongue probing the soft sweetness of her mouth. She melted against him. Justin's hand traced a path down her waist, toward her thigh, then stopped. A part of him held back as sanity returned. *What am I doing? The last thing Lorren needs is for me to take advantage of her. We're both in a highly charged emotional state as a result of the auto accident. I won't be able to handle it if she regrets our lovemaking in the morning.*

Reluctantly, Justin broke off their kiss. "No," he whispered raggedly, forcing his head up. "This is no good."

Misunderstanding his words, Lorren's body stiffened. She pushed herself away from him and his rejection. Humiliation swept through her. She was lying in bed, with her nightgown up, and he didn't want her.

Scott had been right about her.

A fresh wave of pain swept over Lorren. She pushed her gown down and turned away from him. She couldn't look at him. "Please leave," she managed to say, her voice shaky.

Justin got off the bed, straightening his clothes and cursing under his breath. "Lorren, I'm really sorry about—"

"Just leave, Justin." She couldn't handle any words of pity he was about to say.

He hesitated before speaking again, rubbing the palm of his hand across his haggard face. "I think we need to talk about—"

"No. There's nothing to discuss. Just go."

When Lorren heard the door closing behind Justin, she collapsed on the bed, giving in to her tears.

Chapter 6

Justin stood at the grill and basted the ribs. Looking up, he smiled. "Syneda, I'm glad you could make it." He glanced around the patio. "Where's Lorren?"

"She's not coming."

Justin's smile vanished. "Did she say why?"

"She said something about feeling a little under the weather."

Justin cast a sidelong glance through the trees, to the house where Lorren was staying. "Oh, I see."

Syneda was silent for a long moment. As an attorney she'd become very adept at judging people's characters. She felt she'd done a pretty good job of summing up Justin Madaris. He came across as a very caring man, one who would never intentionally hurt a woman. And the bottom line was that Lorren was hurting because she was convinced that, like Scott, Justin had rejected her. Lorren had told her what had almost happened last night, and how Justin had stopped and walked away. She believed he had done so because he'd realized she wasn't worth the bother. But Syneda believed he'd acted the role of a gentleman, and had stopped himself from taking advantage of the situation. Nothing she could say would convince Lorren of her theory. Now Syneda wondered how she could get Justin to succeed where she had failed, without betraying her friend's confidence.

Justin cleared his throat. Syneda was staring at him silently, her sea green eyes oddly speculative. "Is something wrong, Syneda?"

Syneda gazed up at him, her decision made. "Yeah. I have this problem, and I'm hoping you can help me with it."

Justin raised a brow. "Oh, what sort of problem is it?"

"Strictly professional, involving one of my clients. It may be a little out of your expertise, but at times another ear helps. And I'm hoping, with your medical background, you can possibly steer me in the right direction."

"All right. I'll try."

Syneda took a deep breath. "I've been working with this client who's been abused by her husband."

"Physically abused?"

She squinted up at him. "No, emotionally abused."

Justin nodded knowingly. "Sometimes that's even worse. Cruel words can hurt just as deeply as any physical blow. Physical wounds can heal pretty quickly. Mental wounds can fester for years."

"I agree, Justin. My client and her husband have been married a couple of years, and he's managed to tear down her self-confidence as a woman by convincing her she's sexually worthless."

"And she believes him?"

"He's the only man she's ever been involved with, so yes, she believes him. And because he's been successful in convincing her of this, she feels threatened by any other man who tries to get too close."

"In other words, she's built a wall around herself."

"Precisely."

"Sounds like your client has one hell of a problem, Syneda. Have you advised her to seek professional help?"

"Yes, I've tried, but she refuses to listen," Syneda admitted softly. "To be totally honest with you, Justin, I'm not sure professional help is what she needs right now."

Justin lifted a brow. "What do you think she needs?"

"Someone caring and concerned enough to prove her husband wrong."

"Matchmaking isn't within your profession, but if you feel strongly that's the answer, I suggest you do your damnedest to get her out of her present situation by speeding up her divorce. Hopefully she'll be able to rebuild her life. Eventually she'll meet someone who'll realize just how special she is."

Syneda smiled. "Perhaps she has already. She recently moved back to her hometown and has a doctor living close by. In fact, he's her only neighbor, for miles. The good doctor appears to be interested in her. I just hope he's smart enough to key in on the fact she needs his help."

She paused before continuing. "I've met him and, although I really don't know him that well, both my mind and my heart are leading me to believe that he's a good person, and that he won't ever intentionally hurt her. I think he's exactly who she needs now."

She reached out and touched Justin's shoulder. "Thanks for being a captive audience. It felt good to talk to someone else about it."

Justin thought for a long moment before giving her a crooked smile. "You're welcome. You can bend my ear anytime."

Syneda nodded. Satisfied. "Now if you'll excuse me, I'm going to mingle. I see a few people I know over there." She turned to leave.

"Syneda?"

She looked back over her shoulder. "Yes, Justin?"

His eyes met hers directly. "This, ah, client of yours. She sounds like someone who's really a special person."

"She is, Justin. She's a very special person."

"I hope she knows just what a true friend she has in you."

"No, Justin, it's the other way around. I know just what a true friend I have in her. Long ago she was there for me when I was going through a difficult time in my life. And now, I can't stand to see her hurting any longer."

It was strange how things worked out, Justin thought when Syneda walked away. Just a few nights ago, he'd wondered who could provide him with answers to his questions about Lorren. And without even asking, Syneda, in a roundabout way, had told him basically all he needed to know—at the moment. Anything else would have to come directly from Lorren. What he'd found out had explained a lot, especially some of her behavior.

Justin drew in a deep breath. Lorren was the most sensuous woman he'd ever met. How could she discount her worth as a woman? Her ex-husband had really done a number on her.

He leaned against the wooden post and thought of the times he and Lorren had spent together since meeting at Ms. Nora's party—especially last night. When he'd arrived back at her place from the hospital, she had stood in the open door for him. Somehow, she had understood how he'd felt. It was as if she had read his inner thoughts, had known his inner feelings, and had responded to them by offering him comfort and compassion.

He couldn't remember the last time he'd freely

taken either of those things from a woman. But he had accepted them easily from her. By being there for him, she had shared a part of herself, a major concession on her part, and deep down he knew it. He also knew she'd been willing to go further last night. But, somehow, he had found the strength to walk away from her and the complete surrender she had offered.

He had walked away…

Justin took a sharp intake of breath. Did Lorren see his walking away as another rejection? Did she realize that he'd done them both a tremendous favor by pulling back?

He heaved an exasperated sigh. No, she wouldn't realize it. Not in her present frame of mind. She would definitely see it as a rejection.

He ran his hand across his chin. He had to convince Lorren that he hadn't rejected her. Somehow he had to make her understand.

The night air was unusually cool, Lorren thought, stepping out onto her porch. The heavy aroma of smoked spareribs and well-seasoned steamed blue crabs floated on the breeze. The tantalizing smell was coming through the trees from Justin's place.

She should have stayed inside. Unable to concentrate on her writing, she should have done something else, like read a book or watch television. She didn't particularly want to think about Justin tonight; she wanted to think of other things.

But she had nothing else to think about.

Even while sleeping last night, thoughts of him had plagued her. Desire for him had hummed through her body, causing her to shift restlessly in bed, aching for his touch.

A touch she would never feel again.

Smoothing her skirt, she sat down on the bottom step, stretching out her legs. Someone once said, "the truth shall set you free." Well, in her case, learning the truth had placed her in even more bondage. For the first time, she was beginning to think moving back to Ennis had not been such a good idea after all.

She had been a fool to think she could start over. No matter where she went, she couldn't run away from the truth of who she was and what she was. She was a woman with the inability to take care of a man's physical needs. Therefore, she would never be able to share a serious relationship with any man.

Long ago she had learned the best way to protect herself was to stay away from any sort of involvement and to maintain an emotional distance as a safety precaution. She had let her guard down with Justin and was paying for it now. She would have to be more careful in the future. Her peace of mind depended on it.

Justin leaned against the oak tree, glad Lorren hadn't noticed him yet so he could study her. Just looking at her gave him such a sense of pleasure. Lorren Jacobs and her eyes, the color of rich caramel, demanded a second look, and a third. A man would have to be a fool not to appreciate her beauty.

And a man would have to be far worse than a fool not to appreciate her as a woman. Her touch was fire. It rushed through him like a brush blaze caught by the wind. The times they'd kissed, desire, the likes of which he'd never known, pulsed through him, making his need for her insistent and monumental.

But it didn't just stop there. He knew there was more to her than just sensuality and physical beauty.

Lorren was different from any woman he'd been involved with since Denise. From their initial meeting that night, there had been something about her that had drawn him to her like a moth to a flame. And whatever it was, it still held him captured, entranced.

Now, knowing a little about her past life, he could just imagine the pain she had gone through; the misgivings and uncertainties she still felt. For some unexplainable reason, he felt attuned to her and sensitive to her feelings. And he knew, without a doubt, he would not be completely satisfied until all her barriers were gone.

Sighing deeply, he moved away from the tree and began walking toward her.

Lorren sensed someone's presence in the woods and drew in a quick, startled breath.

"I didn't mean to frighten you," Justin said, coming forward.

"Justin?" She sat up straighter, feeling somewhat nervous. "What are you doing here? Why aren't you at the party with your guests?" she asked in a strained voice.

Justin sat down beside her on the wooden step. "Everyone has left except for my brother Clayton and Syneda. And they're too engrossed in a discussion of law to notice my absence. You can't imagine how dull it can be when two attorneys get together."

"Why are you here?"

"I heard you were a little under the weather. Thought I'd drop by to see if there's anything I can do."

"No. I'm fine."

"About last night, Lorren."

"I'd rather not talk about it, Justin."

"That may be true for you, but I need to talk about it."

Lorren stood. "Then talk to yourself, because I don't intend to listen."

Justin reached up and gently touched her arm. "Please, let's talk."

She frowned. This didn't make sense. Why was he here? Now that he knew the truth, he wasn't supposed to come back.

"Please, Lorren," Justin repeated quietly. He wanted to hold her in his arms and protect her from the pain of the past. But first, he had to straighten things out between them.

Something in Justin's voice pulled at Lorren. She

stared at him for a moment before finally giving in and returning to the seat beside him. She firmed her lips. If he wanted to talk, she would let him. For once she wouldn't run away. There was nothing he could say that would be worse than what Scott had already said.

"I owe you an apology for last night, Lorren. I almost pushed you into doing something you weren't ready to do. We were both upset about the accident, and were going to use sex as a way of comforting each other. And as much as I wanted you, that wouldn't have been right. No matter what you might think of me, I would never deliberately take advantage of you. I'm glad we stopped when we did, and I'm sorry I lost control of the situation."

Justin's words left Lorren more than a little stunned. Her lashes flickered, and a cord in her throat tightened. She didn't know what to say. He hadn't pulled away because he'd found her lacking? He had pulled away to not take advantage of her? He had actually wanted her?

"But I thought—"

"Yes? What did you think, Lorren?"

"Nothing. It's not important."

Neither of them spoke for several minutes. Lorren fingered the fabric of her skirt, knowing she should say something. Justin spoke before she had a chance to. "Will you forgive me, Lorren?"

She shrugged. "There's really nothing to forgive,

Justin. What almost happened was just as much my fault, too. As you said, we were both upset and feeling kind of down over the accident. It was just a natural reaction to turn to each other that way."

Lorren felt Justin's arms go around her, and in one smooth sweep, he moved her to his lap. Taken by surprise, she opened her mouth to say something. She couldn't recall what she'd wanted to say when Justin tenderly nestled her in his strong arms.

She could hear the sound of his heartbeat against her face, and could smell the manly scent of him. His chin rested atop her head, his arms wrapped securely around her. His tender hold and the soft stroke of his fingers on her arm were caring. The tensions caused by her jumping to conclusions slowly began leaving her body, and she surrendered to the protectiveness of his embrace, feeling warm and contented.

For a long moment Justin continued to hold her, rocking her gently in his arms. Never before had any man shown her so much tenderness. Never had anything she wanted to feel so wrong felt so right. The feeling was wonderful, but at the same time terrifying. She was attuned to his closeness, his strength, and the hardness of his body. She threw her head back and their eyes met and held. She was startled by the warmth displayed in the depths of his eyes.

"I should go in now, Justin," she whispered. "It's getting late."

Reluctantly, he released her, allowing her to stand. Lorren smoothed down her skirt and straightened her blouse. When she had finished, Justin rose to his feet in a swift, seamless movement and gently pulled her to him. His lips moved in a soft caress, tracing a path across her forehead, the tip of her nose, then across her cheek and to the base of her neck. Leaning over slightly, he touched her mouth very lightly with his.

Lifting his head, he looked down at her. His gaze was gentle. "You do know things aren't completely settled between us, don't you?"

Lorren swallowed and shifted her eyes downward a little. "What do you mean?"

"As I told you before, I'm not into one-night stands. And I'm not interested in a casual entanglement either."

"What exactly are you interested in, Justin?"

"For now, I want to spend some time with you. I want us to get to know each other without your putting up a wall. If you'd like, you can call the shots. We won't do anything you don't want to. I'm willing to take things slow."

Lorren swallowed again. The last thing she needed was to become involved with Justin. But somehow, she felt involved with him already. He was the first man who made her blood race, whose touch stole the very breath from her lungs, and whose kisses made her entire body burn. And he had admitted he wanted her. For those reasons, shouldn't she try discovering more of him? And along with him, shouldn't she try discovering more of herself?

"All right." She trembled when she finally said the words.

Justin's embrace tightened, drawing her closer. "You won't regret it." He wanted to say more, but he didn't.

"So, how was the cookout?"

"It was okay, but you were missed. I know it's kind of late, but I'd like you to meet Clayton. Will you walk with me over to my place?"

Lorren felt tension seep out of her, leaving her oddly relieved and feeling closer to Justin. "Sure, why not. Besides, if we don't put an end to your brother and Syneda's conversation, it might go on forever. She gets kind of fired up whenever she discusses law."

Justin laughed. "So does Clayton. But when I left them, they weren't discussing it, they were debating it. They couldn't seem to agree on any of the issues."

Lorren stuck her hands into the pockets of her skirt as they started walking back toward Justin's place.

Never had she felt this sense of serenity with anyone since her divorce, a sense of well-being Justin could instill so effortlessly.

Wrapping an arm around her shoulder, he pulled her closer to his side. They began walking toward the front of the house. Taking the path through the trees, they headed toward the spot where Justin's brother and Syneda stood in deep conversation.

Lorren could no longer deny she drew comfort from the strong arms around her.

Chapter 7

"She's a girl, Dr. J.!" The little boy with a mop of curly black hair snarled.

"You must be Erick," Lorren replied, trying to hide her grin. Upon opening the door, she'd found Justin with five youngsters surrounding him.

"No, she's not," a brown-eyed boy with toasted skin answered beboppingly. "She's a knockout."

Lorren laughed. "Thanks. And who are you?"

"I'm Charlie. The C in my name stands for *cool.*"

"Oh, all right, Charlie," Lorren said, grinning and turning her attention to the remaining three youngsters. "Now who do we have here?"

"I'm Derick, ma'am. Erick's twin brother," a third little boy answered. "But we're not identical twins," the youngster with close-cropped, curly black hair said shyly.

In more ways than one, Lorren thought, gazing at the mild-mannered Derick, then back at Erick, his surly twin brother, who was eyeing her with distaste.

"I'm Conan," the fourth little boy replied. His oval face was cocoa in color, and his gorgeous ebony eyes matched his tight curly hair. "My friends call me the 'Barbarian.'"

"Oh," Lorren answered as a smile touched her lips. "I'll try remembering that. Who're you?" she asked the remaining little boy with dark brown curly hair who was clinging shyly to Justin's hand. It was obvious he was the youngest of the group. His small bashful face held the innocence of an angel. She fell in love with him at once.

"That's Vincent, ma'am," Derick answered. "He doesn't talk much. He's only five, but Dr. J. always invites him along with us big guys."

Lorren's smile widened. "Hello, Vincent. How are you?"

The little boy cast Justin an uneasy look. Justin nodded his head, then the boy answered softly, "Fine."

"She's not even ready, Dr. J.!" Erick stormed. "Just like a girl to make us have to wait."

"You're wrong, Erick," Lorren chuckled. "I'm ready. I just need help getting my things to the car."

"We don't have a car. Dr. J. brought an RV," Conan quickly corrected her.

"That's right," Lorren replied. "He did mention he would."

"I bet she's bringing a whole bunch of stuff we won't be needing. Girl's stuff. We're going to be crowded out, Dr. J.," Erick stated in disgust.

Lorren tapped her finger thoughtfully to her chin. "In that case I may as well leave behind the huge container full of homemade brownies and cookies I was bringing along."

That statement captured the boys' attention. Justin, who had been quiet all this time, released a hearty laugh. "I was wondering how long it would take you to wrap them around your finger."

Lorren smiled up at him. She hadn't seen him since the cookout Thursday night. He looked handsome as ever. She had never seen such beautiful thick eyelashes on a man before. They were lashes a woman would kill for.

"Hey you guys, this is Lorren Jacobs. She's a friend of mine and will be our special guest for the weekend."

"We've never taken a girl along before, Dr. J.," Erick replied, not bothering to hide his displeasure. "Why is she coming? What makes her so special?"

Complete silence fell upon the group. They eyed both Lorren and Justin speculatively, waiting for Justin's answer. Lorren noticed even Vincent had emerged from his hiding place behind Justin to analyze them.

"First of all, she was kind enough to fill in for Mr. Bob. He couldn't make it this trip. Now, let me see what makes her so special."

Justin then tipped his head to one side as if studying Lorren. "Ummm...she's pretty. Real pretty. She can cook. She understands and likes children, because she writes books especially for them to read. And when you guys get older you'll discover all men like having a girl around every once in a while to keep them in line. I guess all those things make her special."

Lorren felt herself tint from Justin's statement, feeling just as special as he'd made her sound.

"You keep Dr. J. in line?" Charlie asked, as if the task was a monumental undertaking.

Her eyes squinted with laughter. "I try my best."

"Wow!" the boys exclaimed in unison.

Justin laughed. "Come on, you guys. That's enough questions. How about grabbing those things over there and heading on out to the RV. And watch your step."

When the boys were out of hearing range, Justin turned to Lorren. His gaze held her so intently she was only vaguely aware his arm had slipped around her waist. He pulled her against his chest, resting his chin on the top of her head. "Are you ready to have a terrific weekend?"

Lorren took a step back and gazed up at him. "I'm more than ready."

Justin smiled. "Good. John and Juanita should be

there with their group about an hour after we arrive." He extended his hand to her. "Let's go. The guys are waiting."

"Is this a recreational vehicle or an apartment on wheels?" Lorren asked, stepping on board the huge RV and glancing around.

Talk about going camping with all the necessities! It was equipped with a refrigerator and stove, private toilet and shower facilities, a game table, enough room to sleep at least six people comfortably, a disc player, a television and VCR.

Justin chuckled. "I ask myself the same question whenever I'm using it. You may as well make yourself comfortable and enjoy the ride. It'll take a couple of hours to get where we're going."

"When can we start eating the goodies?" Erick asked excitedly licking his lips, his discontent with Lorren's gender suddenly forgotten.

"Not for a while yet. You just finished breakfast. Besides, it's too early for sweets," Justin answered, getting behind the steering wheel and snapping his seat belt in place. "Try keeping yourselves busy until snack time."

"When is snack time?" Charlie asked eagerly.

"Not for at least another hour or so," Justin replied, grinning. Now he understood what his mother meant when she claimed he and his brothers almost ate her out of house and home when they were kids. Little boys seemed to have bottomless pits instead of stomachs.

Apparently satisfied with Justin's answer, the boys, with the exception of Vincent, went toward the back of the RV. Vincent, Lorren noticed, had curled up on one of the sofa-sleepers and was going to sleep. "Vincent isn't very talkative, Justin. Are you sure he's feeling well?" she asked with concern.

"That's just the way he is. He's the newest member of the group, and is still somewhat shy. He's only been with the Society a little over a year, and during that time he's come a long way. He's the lone survivor of an automobile accident that killed both his parents and little sister."

Lorren shuddered as painful memories resurfaced. Her own parents had been killed in a car accident. She would never forget how she, at the age of eight, had taken a final stroll with her parents when she'd walked behind their caskets up the aisle of the church.

"And to make matters worse," Justin continued, "Vincent had no other family. When he first arrived he was scared and withdrawn. He's slowly coming around. I spend more time with him than I do the other boys. He still has a few medical problems as a result of the accident."

"Nothing serious, I hope."

Justin shook his head. "Not anymore. He's coming along nicely."

Lorren met his gaze. "I'm glad you get to spend a lot of time with him, Justin. The worst thing anyone can do is let him continue to withdraw. I went through something similar when I first went to live with Mama Nora and Papa Paul. If it hadn't been for their love and patience, I don't think I could have survived emotionally. It's very hard to adjust when you've lost everyone you've ever loved."

They remained silent for the remainder of the trip until the boys interrupted them for a snack.

They finally reached the campgrounds of Davy Crockett National Forest. Justin delegated the boys the task of unpacking the smaller items from the RV. To Lorren's surprise, the five of them worked well together.

John and Juanita Graham arrived with their group within the hour. Lorren took an immediate liking to the attractive woman who was married to Justin's old college friend.

Juanita had smooth almond skin, high cheekbones, ebony eyes, and a bubbly and friendly smile. Her short curly hair fit almost caplike around her head, emphasizing the beauty of her features and giving her a dark, sultry look, even while dressed in a pair of jeans and an oversize T-shirt.

John, Lorren learned, was a Texas Ranger and was nearly as handsome as Justin, with maple skin and tawny-colored eyes. Before the Grahams left for their own camping site, they had talked Justin and Lorren into making plans for the four of them to get together for dinner sometime in the near future.

It was wonderful to get away and enjoy the solitude

of the wild, Lorren thought. To her dismay, she discovered tremendous pleasure in watching Justin take charge. Dressed in a pair of well-worn jeans that fit his body snugly, and a short-sleeved blue shirt, he looked perfectly at home in his surroundings.

As he worked diligently getting camp set up, Lorren's gaze encompassed his sleek body, the perspiration-sheened brown skin of his bare back after he'd removed his shirt, and the play of muscles across his torso whenever he reached for something.

A couple of times he caught her looking at him and gave her a huge arrogant grin, as if reading her thoughts. She quickly turned her head, embarrassed at being caught, but glanced back at him minutes later.

They spent the rest of the day exploring the park and taking hikes with John, Juanita, and their group. Later that day, Justin, Charlie, and Erick went fishing for their dinner. When they returned Lorren was delegated the task of cooking their catch. She became the hit of the day when she surprised them with a hidden dessert she'd brought along, a huge chocolate cake.

Justin insisted Lorren sleep inside the RV, but she had other ideas and started to protest until Charlie mentioned certain unmentionables, like snakes, bears, and mosquitoes. Justin and the boys really roughed it by bedding down on the ground in sleeping bags with the stars for their roof and a pile of leaves for their pillows.

By the time Lorren settled into the RV that night,

every muscle in her thighs ached, her backside felt sore and her feet were tender. No sooner did her head touch the pillow than she went quickly to sleep.

They awakened early the next morning to Justin's breakfast of biscuits and sausage, hot chocolate for the boys, and coffee for them. It was another full day of vigorous activities. By four o'clock that evening, they were all packed to return home.

Lorren had thoroughly enjoyed herself. The boys, to her surprise and utter amazement, turned out to be a bunch of darlings. They, along with Justin, catered to her every whim. It had been wonderful enjoying the simple pleasures of camping, such as singing songs and exchanging ghost stories over an open fire and hiking in the woods. The camping trip also afforded her an opportunity to see another side of Justin.

She realized just what a genuinely caring man he really was, and saw in him a sensitivity that overwhelmed her. It was evident he loved kids, and the boys adored him. His time had been their time, their survival, his, and their happiness, his enjoyment. She didn't miss the expressions of gaiety on Justin's face when Vincent and Erick recited poems they'd learned in school, or his expression of deep interest as he listened to Conan expound on his desire to one day become an astronaut.

He had hugged Derick with loving arms when he had caught the biggest catch of the day, and had gently but sternly scolded Charlie for his insis-

tence that he be allowed to go spend some time with a group of Girl Scouts he'd discovered camping nearby.

Justin had made them laugh with his rendition of the Fat Albert character. Later, he pulled out a guitar and, ignoring the snickers and giggles from the boys, played her a beautiful love song.

Although there was sexual tension surrounding them on the camping trip, they were able to harness it, most of the time. However, more than once their eyes met over an open fire.

Later that night, when Justin took Lorren home after dropping the boys off, he helped her unload her gear into the house. They worked in silence until the job was done. Afterward, she walked him to the RV.

"Thanks for coming along, Lorren. You were a big hit with the boys, and I thoroughly enjoyed your company."

"Thanks for inviting me. I had a great time. The boys were wonderful, and John and Juanita are really super people."

Justin nodded. "Are you planning to go to the National Polka Festival?"

"Yes."

"Are you going with anyone?"

"No."

"Would you go with me?"

Lorren smiled. "Do you promise to bring me straight home afterward?"

Justin chuckled. "If you insist, but you have to

admit our being at Bristol Trail may have been a blessing for those two kids."

Lorren shuddered slightly, remembering the accident. Earlier Justin had given her an update on the teenagers' conditions. Although improved, their conditions were still guarded. "Maybe it was at that."

"Well, I better get along. I need to return the RV tonight. I guess I'll see you later."

"Okay."

Justin stepped closer. Lorren gazed up at his face, just a couple of inches above hers. He gently pulled her to him. "How do you manage to stay slim and trim when you bake so well?" He placed his arms around her slender waist and drew her closer.

Her response was an amusing laugh. "I usually don't bake for myself. I enjoy baking for other people." She unconsciously wrapped her arms around his neck. He didn't seem as surprised at her boldness as much as she did.

"You can bake for me anytime," he said huskily, before bringing his lips to hers. His tongue sought hers, tentative at first, then with more assurance when he felt her response.

As their mouths clung together, his hands pulled her body closer to him. Moments later he reluctantly pulled away. "Yes sirree, you can bake for me anytime," he whispered in between quick breaths.

Lorren smiled. "I'll remember that."

"How about joining me in a late-night swim when I get back?" he suggested in a deep husky voice.

She moistened her lips with her tongue as a tingling sensation settled in the pit of her stomach from his touch. She shook her head. "I don't think that's a good idea."

His hand brushed her cheek. Dark eyes met hers. "I happen to think it's a great idea."

Lorren smiled, feeling the gentle pressure of his hand on her face. She was tempted to turn her head and touch the tip of her tongue against his fingers. Instead she said, "You would be the one to think so. If my memory serves me correctly, the one and only time we went swimming together, you didn't play fair."

Justin laughed. "*I* didn't play fair? Lady, *you* give a whole new meaning to the word cheat."

"I do not."

"Oh, yes you do."

Lorren stuck her tongue out at him. Justin quickly captured it with his mouth, all firm with need. Lorren felt fire race down to her toes and back, settling in the core of her.

She moaned deep in her throat as she gave herself up to Justin's touch and taste. His hand wandered up and down, caressing first her hips through the fabric of her shorts, then her bottom.

The kiss continued for a long moment until, breathless, Justin drew back. "Lorren Jacobs, you're going to be the death of me yet."

She gazed up at him with eyes alive with desire. "Why do you say that?"

"Because I want you so much I could die."

"Oh, Justin." Lorren curled into him, wrapping her arms around his waist and resting her head upon his chest. "You really mean that, don't you?" Disbelief, then acceptance, was in her voice.

Her words, spoken in a heartfelt whisper, tore through Justin. It was hard to believe that a woman so beautiful and desirable could harbor insecurities about herself and her ability to be wanted by a man.

"Yes, baby. I really meant it. Trust me."

He pulled Lorren closer in his embrace until every inch of his body touched every available inch of hers. His body shook with the intensity of the emotions he felt inside. They stood that way for an endless length of time.

"Lorren," Justin breathed, lifting her face with one of his fingers under her chin, "I told you the other night I was willing to take things slow. I meant it then, but now I want to say the hell with slowness. And unless you're in agreement with me, I suggest you go on into the house."

Lorren pushed away from Justin's chest and looked up into his eyes. Without saying anything, she slowly turned and walked away. When she got halfway to the door, she turned around. Justin was leaning against the RV, with one foot crossed over the other at the ankle and folded arms across his chest. His eyes were directly on her, watching her intently.

She knew her lips were swollen and must look a

sight, but nonetheless, she tilted them in a smile. "Justin?"

"Yes?"

"There's always tomorrow."

Justin nodded, returning her smile. He dared not hope her words were hinting at possibilities of things yet to come.

Lorren turned and hurried on inside.

Justin kept his gaze on Lorren until she'd entered the house and locked the door behind her. He took a deep, calming breath before reaching for the doorknob on the RV.

"Yeah, there's always tomorrow," he said softly.

Chapter 8

Lorren couldn't sleep.

The soft spattering rain could be heard beating gently against the window, and not too far away the sound of distant thunder rumbled across the sky. However, it wasn't the weather keeping her awake. She couldn't get Justin out of her mind.

Sighing, she slid out of bed and crossed the room. Turning on one of the small lamps on the dresser, she stared at her reflection in the mirror. She looked, she admitted, like the same woman who had arrived in Ennis a couple of weeks ago. But she realized something was different, something not showing that was deep within.

She had fallen in love.

Lorren had sworn after her experience with Scott, she would never fall prey to that emotion again, but somehow what she'd merely shrugged off as a physical attraction to Justin had been transformed into love. Genuine love. And with that startling clarity, she could now admit that what she'd felt for Scott was nothing compared to what she was feeling for Justin.

Straightening, she switched off the lamp and got back into bed. Lying in darkness, she gazed up at the ceiling, reflecting on her relationship with Justin. In a little more than a few days she had gained so much insight into who he was as a man, a doctor, and a person. She had dated Scott for eight months before they had married, and had never really known him or what he'd been capable of doing until it had been too late.

Her ragged sigh echoed in the quiet stillness of the room. Even though Justin had admitted he believed in love, he didn't love her. Lorren knew she was merely someone he was spending time with while waiting patiently for that special woman he believed fate would deliver to him.

She had been hurt too deeply in the past to allow herself to assume that, although Justin enjoyed her friendship, company, and the growing passion between them, he wanted more. She was determined never to make the same mistake with him that she'd made with Scott by assuming too much.

A lone tear fell from Lorren's eye, making its

way down her cheek. Would love always be something she could touch but never hold on to?

The gentle sound of the rain soon lulled Lorren. Her lashes fluttered against her cheeks as the heaviness of sleep touched her.

The roar of thunder grew louder. Lorren awoke, startled, hearing the torrential rain pounding against the window. Lightning flashed everywhere.

Gripping the bedcovers, she battled with fear, not of the storm but the memories it seemed to evoke. Severe thunderstorms often made her remember the night her parents had gotten killed. And tonight, the memories were stronger than ever.

Drawing the covers around her, she scrunched deeper into the pillows. Howling winds beat against the windows and jagged streaks of lightning tormented the sky. Lorren covered her ears with her hands to drown out the perilous noise. She didn't want to remember.

Justin's words filtered through her mind. *Don't forget I'm next door if you need anything. No matter how late it is...*

Unable to confront the memories any longer, she jumped out of bed, shoved on her slippers, and grabbed her robe. Dismissing the danger, she ran from the house into the pouring rain to the one person she needed most.

She ran to Justin.

* * *

Justin groaned as he pulled the pillow over his head in an attempt to drown out the incessant knocking at his door. He was too absorbed in his dream to be distracted.

...Silken arms reached up to encircle his neck as he captured eager lips in a seductive kiss. He released her mouth momentarily to drink in the beauty of her naked brown body. Desire surged through him each time he looked at her. Caramel-colored eyes, aflame with a heated hunger; gazed back at him. He rose above her, proud and powerful, wanting to be tender, yet desperately wanting to be inside her...

The knocking became more persistent as reality invaded the deep recesses of his mind and abruptly ended his dream. Struggling to throw off the covers, he groped for his pajama bottoms and hurriedly put them on. Who in their right mind would venture out at this ungodly hour of the night and in this wretched weather? He left the bedroom and muttered an obscenity when his toe came in contact with the coffee table, Limping, he finally reached the door and yanked it open.

"Lorren!" His surprise was immediately replaced by concern. Her nightclothes were drenched, and she shook from head to toe. At first he thought the cause was the chilling rain, then he saw the terror in her eyes and face.

"What's the matter? Baby, what's wrong?"

Petrified caramel eyes pleaded understanding.

"I—I…the storm…I don't want to remember," she answered incoherently. Her voice was a mere whisper before the flash of a jagged spear of lightning and the sound of a mighty roar of thunder propelled her into his arms.

Justin held her tight against him, not caring he was getting soaked in the process. Cradling her tenderly in his arms, he picked her up. After kicking the door shut, he carried her into his bedroom. Gently placing her in a huge recliner near the bed, he knelt beside her. Softly stroking wet hair from her face he said, "It's okay. You're here with me. You're safe."

Her eyes fluttered open. She gazed down at him.

"Are you all right, Lorren?"

She closed her eyes, remembering another time when she had run out into the storm at night. She nodded weakly, still trembling.

"You need to get out of these wet things, take a hot shower, and dry your hair. Do you think you can manage by yourself, or do you need my help?"

Their eyes met. Justin's expression was one of genuine concern and caring. Lorren's lids lowered. "I—I can manage, but…" She swallowed deeply. "I don't have anything else to put on."

"Don't worry about that. I'll find something." He tenderly caressed her cheek. "Everything's going to be all right."

The touch of Justin's finger on her skin brought a sensation of warm security. His eyes held hers with mesmerizing intensity.

"I'll leave you alone. Everything you need should be in there," he said, indicating the bathroom.

She nodded.

"I'll be right outside the door if you need me." He stood and walked out of the room, closing the door behind him.

Lorren felt totally drained, both mentally and physically. Justin's voice had been kind, almost loving. Sighing deeply, she stood to go into the bathroom.

In the living room, Justin paced the floor from one end to the other. After a while, he sat on the sofa, with his elbows resting on his thighs and his hands clasped loosely between his knees. He stared thoughtfully into space.

What was there about the storm that had frightened her so much to have driven her out into it? And what was it that she didn't want to remember?

When he heard Lorren moving about in the other room, he decided to fix something hot and soothing for her to drink. She'd need it after being out in the weather.

Lorren came out of the bathroom, securely wrapped in one of Justin's oversize bath towels. She was glad the storm had subsided. Entering the bedroom, she saw a Houston Texans T-shirt lying on the bed. Discarding the towel, she slipped into the big shirt. Her slender form was swallowed by it as it fell past her knees.

She glanced around the room. Shades of sable

brown, black, and tan filled it with masculine strength and sensuality.

Above the king-size bed hung a colossal African painting depicting intricate expressions of cultural pride. Numerous pieces of artwork by various African-American artists adorned the other walls in the room. A tall bookcase stood on one side, neatly filled to capacity with books, carvings, and figurines.

Like a kid turned loose in the toy department, she padded barefoot to the bookcase for a closer look. She was impressed with Justin's collection of Buffalo Soldier figurines honoring the elite band of black soldiers who served in the Union Army over a century ago. She could tell the figurines had been skillfully hand-painted.

Lorren knew she should go out to the living room and face Justin. But at the moment she couldn't cope with an explanation. She wondered what he thought of her? Did he think she was a madwoman for being out in the storm? A soft knock sounded on the door, interrupting her thoughts.

"Lorren?"

"Yes, come in. I'm dressed."

Justin entered the room. "I've brought you something hot to drink, love." He handed her the cup.

Love? Lorren tossed the word of endearment about in her mind. *Love, baby, honey, sweetheart, sugar, darling*—all were words Scott had used all the time without any particular significance. "Thanks, and I know you're wondering why I was out in the storm..."

"We'll talk later. Right now I want you to take a swallow of that. It'll warm you up a bit."

Nodding, she took a sip, then frowned.

Justin grinned sheepishly at her. "I put some whiskey in it. After being out in this weather, you need it."

Lorren smiled back, then took another sip.

"You should try to get some sleep. I'll be out in the living room."

"I can't take your bed. I'm all right now. I'll go back to—"

"No. You're more than welcome to stay here. The sofa will do me just fine. Try getting some rest. We'll talk some more in the morning." Turning, he started out of the door.

"Justin?"

He turned around. "Yes?"

"Thanks."

He smiled. "Anytime." He closed the door behind him.

Lorren finished the rest of her drink and placed the cup on the nightstand. She then pushed the covers back and slid into the roomy bed, settling comfortably. The clean masculine scent of Justin clung to the sheets, pillows, and bedcovers. She found safety and warmth in the manly fragrance. Shifting her head on the pillow, she was soon sound asleep.

Lying on the sofa in the darkened living room, Justin studied the closed door. "I'm glad one of us can sleep," he muttered, shifting positions again. He tried not to think about the transparency of Lorren's wet nightclothes when she'd first arrived, or her in his bed with his T-shirt as her only piece of clothing. Much to his dismay, the thoughts made his pulse race, and a shiver rippled through him.

His mind then voiced the questions it had earlier. What had driven her out in the storm? And what was it she didn't want to remember? Did either have anything to do with that creep she'd been married to? Whatever was bothering her, she was enduring her own private storm.

Justin willed himself to be patient. He would get answers to his questions tomorrow. Pounding his pillow into a more comfortable shape, he turned over, hoping he'd be able to get some sleep.

In the deep recesses of her dream-ravaged sleep, Lorren struggled to free herself from her dream, crying out at the fear holding her in its grip. Thrashing about, she kicked her covers aside.

"Lorren," a gentle masculine voice called out to her. She felt strong arms engulfing her. Slowly her heart slowed its wild race. Forcing her eyes open, she saw that Justin was with her. He was half-kneeling, half-bending at her bedside. Tightening her arms she clung to him, her body ripped by uncontrollable spasms.

Justin's hands stroked her hair, back, and shoulders. "It's all right, sweetheart," he whispered softly as she became calmer. "You were having a bad dream. It's okay. I wasn't far away."

Lorren tried to stop trembling. Tonight she'd had a full-blown replay of that night eighteen years ago, when her world had come to an end. "Oh, Justin," she whispered against his throat. "I relived that night."

He kissed the tears from her eyes. "What night?"

"The night my parents left me." Her voice broke slightly. "It was a night very much like tonight. We were having the worst thunderstorm I'd ever seen. I was eight years old and had gone to bed. My parents had gone out for the evening and had left me in the care of a baby-sitter."

She paused to catch her breath. "The thunder couldn't smother the sound of the doorbell ringing later that night. I got up and saw two policemen talking to my baby-sitter. I overheard them telling her my parents had been killed in a car accident on the way home."

She trembled at the memory. "I screamed and, before anyone could stop me, I ran out into the storm."

Justin tenderly stroked her hair. His heart went out to the child who'd overheard such shocking news. He could just imagine her emotional turmoil. "Where did you go?"

She shrugged. "Nowhere in particular. I just kept running and running. It seemed I ran forever before one of the policemen caught up with me."

Justin held her tighter in his arms. "But tonight, when you ran out into the storm, you went somewhere, Lorren. You came here to me." He made a move to stand. "You should try sleeping now."

Lorren's hold on him tightened. "Don't…don't leave me, please, I don't want to be alone. Not now."

Justin only hesitated a moment before slipping into bed beside her, gathering her into his arms. "Go on and get some sleep. I'm here with you."

Releasing a sigh, she let her eyes flutter closed, feeling safe in the arms of the man she loved.

Justin forced himself to remain still while he held Lorren. Perspiration formed on his forehead. He was fighting a feverish desire to make love to her. The memory of the erotic dream he'd been having moments before she'd arrived didn't help matters.

A moan got trapped in his throat when she shifted positions in his arms, bringing a firm flat stomach and full breasts against him. His fingers itched to lift up the T-shirt and explore every part of her body, beginning with the very essence of her womanhood.

He closed his eyes, as if doing so would shut her from his mind as well as from his sight, and would bring his thoughts under control. Even though this was definitely the place for what he longed to do to her, now was certainly not the time. The last thing she needed was to be taken advantage of.

He opened his eyes seconds later. Tonight would be a long night. *A very long night.*

Consciousness slowly infiltrated Lorren's mind, and her eyes gradually opened. Justin was lying next to her, asleep. His hand was resting on the curve of her hip, and her head was cradled against his shoulder. She could feel the taut hardness of one of his legs, which was thrown over hers.

She lay perfectly still for a moment as memories of her dream came flooding back. The last thing she remembered was falling asleep in Justin's arms.

Swallowing nervously, she fixed her eyes on the man who held her securely in his warm embrace. To wake up in his arms gave her a deep feeling of warmth and contentment, but it didn't completely erase her uneasiness.

Justin stirred slightly. His eyes suddenly flickered open and held hers. That one instant of eye contact jolted Lorren, making her heart take a perilous leap, and spurring a heated sensation in the pit of her stomach. He continued to stare at her, his fixed gaze like a soft caress. She could feel the touch of that gaze and tried to throttle back the dizzying current racing through her.

Desire, the likeness of which she'd never known, rose in her like the hottest fire, clouding her mind and heating the soft core of her body. It was as if his eyes were casting a spell on her, bewitching her senses. She was transfixed, mesmerized by a fascination so overwhelming, so overpowering, it acted like a catalyst destroying her self-restraint.

Accepting her dilemma was both frightening and exhilarating, and with the steamy mist floating around her, from whence there was no escape, she faced the truth. She wanted to make love with him.

All her uncertainties melted into a driving need to discover what lay ahead in an intimate union.

They continued to stare at each other it seemed for the longest time. Then Justin's mouth captured hers. He kissed her softly at first, a series of slow, shivery kisses. Suddenly, he began smothering her lips with demanding mastery and pulled her closer to him.

Her mouth opened invitingly, accepting his probing tongue. Her surrender was instantaneous as she returned his urgent searing kisses. She kissed him in all the ways he had ever kissed her.

Justin inwardly berated himself for coming on so fast and so strong, but he didn't want to give her the chance to think about anything except what was taking place between them.

His hands sought the hem of the oversize T-shirt, and, breaking the kiss, he gently pulled it up and over her head, removing it completely. He quickly resumed kissing her.

Lorren moaned in his mouth when his finger traced a line around her navel before slowly moving upward to her breasts. His hands tenderly cupped their fullness. In one smooth movement, his tongue replaced his fingers on her breasts, bringing their dark tips to crested peaks.

Moments later, she uttered a small cry of pleasure when his hands were on the move again, gliding over her, as though obsessed with knowing every line of her body.

He stroked her back and shoulders, squeezed her

behind, and spanned her waist and thighs. When his hand moved lower to the very essence of her, little whimpers of pleasure escaped her throat, only to be captured by his mouth.

Lorren's mind was whirling. Sensations she'd never felt before tore through her body. All she could think about was the feel of his sensual mouth and hands on her, making her tremble with a foreign need.

She became totally lost in a blaze of passion and gave herself over to all the things he was making her feel. She forgot everything except Justin and his touch. She couldn't think of anything else.

"Stop me now if you don't want things to go any further. Because if you don't, I won't be able to stop later. I want you too much, Lorren."

Each word he spoke sounded like a caress, an erotic stroke. Lorren wanted him, too. She couldn't deny she was aching with a need to be possessed by him.

"Tell me, Lorren. Tell me what you want me to do."

She answered, whispering in his ear, "I want you to make love to me."

Justin didn't realize until that very moment how much he longed to hear those words from her. Standing, he removed his pajama bottoms, his eyes never leaving hers.

Moments later he was completely naked. His rich brown body was totally male, totally splendid, and, at the moment, totally aroused…for her.

He sought out her lips when he rejoined her in bed, pulling her to him. "I've wanted you for so long,

Lorren. From the first moment I saw you that night, I wanted you," he breathed hotly against her ear.

He kissed and caressed every inch of her body. She became a writhing mass of red-hot passion from the heat his touch generated. He was losing himself in a sensual whirlwind, but knew he had to take the necessary steps so there wouldn't be any regrets later. He tore his lips from hers. "Baby, are you protected?"

She shook her head, answering in a breathless whisper as shivers coursed through her. "I—I, there was never a need..."

Justin reached into a drawer of the nightstand and withdrew a small foil packet. "I'll protect you," he said huskily.

Lorren trembled with the force of her emotions as she watched him prepare himself for her. A short while later he came back to her. Their limbs automatically tangled, all control lost.

Lorren's passion-engulfed mind felt his knees nudge open her thighs, his hand parting her, his body moving over her, and the hardness of him probing at the heat of her, pressing downward and slowly penetrating her. She sucked in her breath at the sheer size of him.

She cried out his name the moment their bodies became one. The fullness and strength of him was deep inside her, and she curved her body receptively.

"Are you all right, love?" he asked tenderly, giving her body time to adjust to him. Her body felt hot and tight.

She smiled up at him, her face damp with perspiration. "I've never felt so alive, so filled with wanting, so filled with need..."

"Neither have I," he rasped.

Placing a kiss on her lips, he slowly and gently began moving within her, setting an erotic rhythm.

Lorren wrapped her legs around him. Her lips moved reflexively, keeping time with his movements as he burrowed deeper and deeper inside her. His tongue, seeking hers, matched the rhythm of their bodies.

Justin murmured softly in her ear with each sensual stroke into her body. He told her how good her mouth tasted, how wonderful she felt to him, and just how incredible she was making him feel.

"Explosive," he breathed against her lips. "You're explosive, sweetheart. I can't get enough of you. Baby, you are completely blowing my mind."

The feel of Lorren moving beneath him brought on memories of the night of Ms. Nora's party, when he'd watched her on the dance floor, moving her body to the sound of the music. He could feel the increasing tempo of her hips moving to meet his every stroke, beat for beat. Her sighs and moans were music to his ears, a sensuously sweet melody that caused one feverish sensation after another to overtake him.

"I don't think I can handle too much more of this," he said, groaning, fighting for control. He pushed harder and deeper into the moist, clinging heat of her. "Baby, you're too much."

Lorren's senses were on overload and his words, spoken in a guttural groan, pushed her over the edge. She gripped his shoulders and dug her nails into his skin, feeling his muscles strain and tighten against her hands. With all the strength she could muster, she kept up with him and his vigorous pace. Each hard, powerful stroke into her body was intense, ecstatic, complete. She gave just the response his body demanded, making their movements more wild and feverish.

"You're perfect." Justin breathed the words into her mouth as he surged forward one last time. His cry of satisfaction muffled against her mouth the moment his body bucked and spasmed with his release.

Their passion encompassed them. Together they scaled the heights of ecstasy, becoming one in body and soul.

Lorren cried.

She couldn't stop the tears flowing down her cheeks and the hard sobs shaking her body.

Justin cradled her face between his hands, alarmed. "Baby…Lorren, sweetheart. What's wrong? Did I hurt you?"

Lorren lifted her tear-stained face to meet him. The expression in his eyes showed such open concern and tenderness. It made her cry even more.

He gathered her closer to him as she wept, crying her heart out in harsh, racking sobs that shook her body.

"Please, Lorren. Answer me. Did I hurt you?"

"I—I never…I never knew anything could—could be so…so beautiful," she cried brokenly. "I never knew I—I could feel that way. Or that—that I could make anyone feel the way you—you said I made you feel." She turned her face into his bare chest. "Oh, Justin, I never knew."

Justin expelled a ragged breath. He was glad her tears weren't from any physical pain he'd inflicted. But he knew of the emotional pain Syneda had hinted at—the one caused by her ex-husband. He wanted her to share that pain with him, so he could help rid her of it.

"Talk to me, Lorren. You've been married before. How could you not have known?"

Lorren raised tear-filled eyes to him. "Scott told me I—I was a failure in bed. He said I was lacking. And until a few minutes ago," she whispered brokenly, "until we made love, I—I was certain it was the truth. But he lied, Justin. He lied to me. How could he have hurt me that way?"

Justin hugged her tightly to him. "Oh, sweetheart, the only one who has an answer to that question is him. Chances are he lied to hide his own feelings of failure. It wasn't you who was lacking, but him. Instead of admitting that to himself, he found it easier to cast the blame on you."

He rested his cheek on the top of her head. If her ex-husband was around this very minute, he would do the man in for what he'd done to her.

"He lied to you, Lorren. Trust me." Justin shifted positions, and she could feel the heat of him, rigid from wanting her again. "See how quickly and easily my body responds to you. Feel pride in your power as a woman, your ability to bring pleasure this way. You did more than just live up to my expectations. You went above and beyond my wildest dream. Nothing could have prepared me for what we shared. Nothing. I feel like I've been to heaven and back. It's not the act of lovemaking itself that makes it special, but the person you share it with. Making love with you was special. It was earth-shattering, and something I could never forget."

Lorren knew she would never feel more like a woman or love Justin more than she did at that very moment. In his arms she had learned what it was to make love, truly make love.

Their eyes met and held for a long, silent moment before Justin leaned over, parted her lips with his tongue, and eased inside. Her arms went around his neck as she drew his tongue deeper into her mouth, then gave hers to him.

Love, strong and deep, swelled within Lorren, and Justin once again went about transporting her to a world of indescribable beauty and passion.

The moon reached out and grappled a dark cloud for possession of what remained of the night.

The storm was over.

Justin drew a long breath and slowly expelled it.

Lorren was nestled up against him, asleep in his arms. He gazed down tenderly at her, studying the warm sensual glow of peace on her face. With care, not wanting to wake her, he slid his arms around her, gently bringing her closer to him.

He stared at her in awed wonder. Never in his life had making love with anyone been so powerful, so magnificent, so intoxicating, so satisfying.

Never.

He turned his head away—from looking at her with the admission that that included his lovemaking with Denise.

The truth hammered into him with all the force of a tidal wave. What he'd always believed to be the ultimate in sexual fulfillment in the arms of the woman he'd loved and married didn't come close to what he had experienced tonight with Lorren.

And that realization shook him to the core, because he didn't know if perhaps his lovemaking with Denise wasn't as exciting as it could have been, or if making love with Lorren was going far beyond anything he thought possible.

He had loved Denise, both physically and emotionally, in a gentle kind of way. The passions he'd shared tonight with Lorren had been wild and feverish.

A knot formed in his throat as he looked down at the gold coin medallion resting on his naked chest. It was his visible, tangible bond to Denise.

In sleep, Lorren's tousled head lay against the medallion. Earlier, her tears had bathed it when she'd cried. A part of him had known the exact moment of contact.

It was that part of him that had reached out to Lorren when she had needed to be comforted.

It was that inner part of him no other woman had touched since Denise.

It was his heart.

Chapter 9

Pulling on a pair of jeans, Justin couldn't help gazing down at Lorren, asleep in his bed, bathed in the warm glow of the morning light. A mass of glossy dark brown hair framed her face and shoulders, making her even more beautiful.

His gaze lingered on the dark tips of her bare breasts for an instant, before leaning over to cover her completely with the bedspread.

He left the bedroom for the kitchen. After a night of vigorous lovemaking, he had a ferocious appetite. It took only a few minutes to get the coffee started, then he went back and checked on Lorren. Finding her still asleep, he returned to the kitchen to phone his office, hope riding high on this call. His first patient, Mrs. Breland, was due in the office at eleven, but was notorious for last-minute cancellations.

Moments later, Justin hung up the phone, smiling. Mrs. Breland hadn't failed him. His first appointment was not until one o'clock. That would give him extra time to spend with Lorren before he'd have to leave.

There were a lot of questions concerning their relationship floating around in his mind. He needed answers. He'd lain awake most of the night, trying to figure out what sort of relationship he wanted with Lorren and what sort of relationship she would agree to. All he was sure of at the moment was that he wanted her.

And he wanted her badly. He was afraid to look at the possibilities beyond that one emotion.

The smell of coffee brought Lorren instantly awake. Opening her eyes, she found herself in bed alone. She sucked in a deep breath as memories of Justin's lovemaking filtered through her mind. It had been the most beautiful thing she'd ever experienced.

On her wedding night, Scott's performance should have forewarned her of his downright selfish nature. The lovemaking had been rushed and totally unfulfilling for her. It had left her wondering what all the fuss over making love had been about.

Now she knew.

Justin had been right. It wasn't the act itself that made it special, but the person you shared it with.

The thought that she'd pleased Justin filled her with a multitude of emotions—joy, delight, and relief. The sexual gratification he'd experienced with her had been real, and she was still in awe of it. His body had been warm and hard, and his whole being had vibrated under her touch.

He'd burrowed deeper and deeper inside of her, whispering words in her ear, letting her know just how good she made him feel. He'd released a loud moan before climaxing with her name on his lips. They'd made love over and over, their hunger for each other insatiable.

"You look like you belong in my bed."

Lorren turned her head in the direction of the deep, sexy masculine voice. Justin stood shirtless in the doorway of the bedroom. Lorren's mouth went dry as her gaze raked his dark muscular body. He was such a good-looking man—in or out of his clothes.

Sauntering over to the bed wearing jeans that clung to his body like a second skin, he knelt on the bed, drawing her to him. His long hard kiss left her weak, filled with need and desire. She wrapped her arms around his neck when he pulled her closer to him.

"We need to talk, Lorren. About us."

Lorren nodded, unable at the moment to say anything. Held within the circle of his arms, she gazed into his dark eyes. She felt too weak after the kiss they'd shared to speak.

A fresh jolt of sensual shocks raced through her

when Justin's fingers threaded through the thickness of her hair, tightening around the silken strands.

"I want you, Lorren. I want you to be mine," he whispered. His hand leisurely stroked her body, sensitizing every inch of her skin.

Lorren sucked in her breath sharply at the feel of his hands on her. She allowed her mind to zero in on the words he'd spoken. He wanted to claim her as his. But not forever, and not as the woman he loved or wanted to marry. He wanted her to be his, the woman he could share his passion with.

Tell him you love him, an inner voice urged. *Tell him you're no longer afraid to want all the things he believes in. Tell him how he's single-handedly destroyed your resolve against love and marriage. Tell him you're no longer confused about what you want in life, as long as that life includes him.*

Another part of her mind screamed, *Girl, don't be a fool! He hasn't said anything that should make you think he wants more than what he's asking for. All he wants is an affair, not a lifetime commitment. And if he thinks you're getting too attached, he may back off. Then you'll be alone again. Remember what he told you. Even though he sanctions love and marriage, he believes in fate, and that one day the special woman he's holding out for will eventually come into his life. He hasn't given any indication that he thinks you're the one, so just appreciate the time the two of you'll share until things come to an end.*

Justin stilled Lorren from any further thoughts

when he captured her face in his hands, making her gaze into his eyes. The look in them was a mixture of passion and tenderness.

"I have to know you *won't* put roadblocks between us again tomorrow. I need to know for sure, Lorren."

The force of Justin's gaze swept through Lorren, making her want to scream out the depth of her feelings for him. Speechlessly, breathlessly, she shook her head.

"Say it, Lorren. I want to hear it from your lips. Tell me you're mine."

Mixed emotions filled Lorren. He was asking for a commitment. A commitment without a future. A commitment until he had his fill of her. Could she handle that? She would be entering into a relationship with him with both eyes wide open and her heart on a platter.

Moving her fingers gently over the slight roughness of his unshaven jaw, with her heart in her throat she answered, "Yes, Justin. I'm yours."

Justin hadn't realized he'd been holding his breath until Lorren's words were said, her commitment to him spoken. He pulled her to him, sealing their mouths together.

Lorren was instantly lost, as she became wrapped up in the feel of his mouth on hers. Uttering a soft moan, she kissed him back, meeting his tongue, tasting him, and drawing him into her more deeply, hungrily.

He slowly released her and stood back from the bed. Lorren watched as he unzipped his pants and slowly began removing them.

"Aren't you going into the office today?" she asked in a whisper of her own voice, watching him discard his jeans.

"My first appointment isn't due until one. If an emergency comes up, Sandra will call me." He smiled down at her. "Let's forget about everything and just concentrate on us."

Lorren returned his smile when Justin came back to the bed. Tossing the covers aside, he slipped in next to her, gathering her in his arms.

"Oh, Justin. I feel so wonderful. It's hard to describe in words just how I feel. Years ago, the Stylistics came out with a song titled, 'You Make Me Feel Brand-New.' That's a perfect way to describe just how you've made me feel, brand-new."

Justin leaned over and gave her a kiss…and more.

Hours later, Lorren's mouth curved into a lazy, satisfied smile. "What time is it?"

Justin pulled up his jeans and turned around. "Close to eleven."

"I've never stayed in bed this late."

Justin laughed in sheer joy at the expression on her face. "Maybe you never had a reason to before. I'm going to fix a light brunch. That should hold us both over until we go out tonight."

Lorren raised a brow. "We're going out?"

"I thought it'd be nice. There's a super restaurant in Dallas I'd like to take you to. But if you'd rather, we could stay here and get into other things," he hinted suggestively, coming to stand before the bed.

Lorren shifted slightly in bed and moistened her swollen lips with her tongue. "Going out tonight will be fine. I'd like to take a shower now. Do you have another T-shirt I can borrow?"

"Yeah. There should be another one in that top drawer over there. How do you feel?"

"Sore," she answered honestly.

"That's understandable. We'll have to do something about that. Go on and take your shower. I'll have brunch prepared by then." He left the room.

Lorren had been in the shower for a few minutes when the shower door opened, exposing a completely naked Justin. "Justin! What are you doing?" she squealed.

In answer, he stepped into the shower, closing the door behind him. He cornered her nude body between his and the shower wall, pressing her against the ceramic tile, and pulling her into his arms.

"I'm going to make love to you, here in the shower. The use of your muscles, together with the warm water, will work the soreness out of your body," he answered, reaching behind her to retrieve the soap from its compartment.

Lorren's eyes widened. "Make love in here? But how?"

"Like this." He proceeded to do wonderful things

to her body as he introduced her to the various ways of lovemaking. Ways Lorren didn't know could be done in a shower or anywhere else.

The restaurant Justin had chosen for dinner was an elegant establishment that spared no expense in creating an atmosphere catering to the tastes of the affluent. They were shown to a table that had a fantastic view of downtown Dallas.

"Justin, you didn't have to go out of your way for dinner tonight," Lorren said after the waiter had taken their order.

A grin tilted his lips. "I want tonight to be just as special as today was. This is just an example of the many things to come. I would, however, like to ask a favor of you."

Lorren lifted an arched eyebrow as a smile touched her lips. "Another camping trip already?"

Justin laughed. "No, not another camping trip. Do you remember my mentioning I'd purchased the Taylors' place and was completely renovating it?"

"Yes, I remember."

Justin took a sip of his wine. "Well, I seem to have encountered a little problem."

"What?"

"The interior designer dropped by the house with catalogs of material and fabric samples before I picked you up. I'm at a loss as to what to select. So I was wondering if you'd help me out."

"How?"

"I'd like you to meet with the interior designer for me and give her some suggestions."

Surprised by his request, she said, "But I don't know what you may or may not like."

One corner of Justin's mouth lifted in a satisfied grin. "I'll like whatever you select."

Absorbing his words, she bit her lower lip. How could he ask her to help decorate a house he would one day share with Ms. Fate, his future wife? A woman she'd already begun to hate. "I don't know, Justin. Did you think of asking one of your sisters, or maybe your mom?"

Justin sensed her hesitation. "Why can't you do it?"

"Why can't one of them?"

"I'd like you to."

Lorren sighed heavily. "I don't think that would be fair to the woman you'll one day bring there as your wife. How would she feel, knowing her home had been decorated by a woman with whom you once had an affair?" There, she'd said it. She had to be realistic that one day their relationship would end.

Justin started to tell her the reason he wanted her to do it was because he desired something of her in his home, something to remind him daily of her. But he couldn't bring himself to say the words. "If she has a problem with it, she can redo it."

Lorren lowered her lashes. She couldn't let him know how much his words had pierced her heart. Those weren't the words she had wanted to hear. "All right. If you really feel that way about it, I'll be more than happy to meet with the interior designer for you."

He smiled. "Thanks, Lorren."

There was little conversation between them when Justin drove her home. It seemed they were both deep in their own private thoughts. Every so often he would give her a smile, bestowing upon the car's interior a challenging intimacy.

The evening had made Lorren realize just how tenuous and fragile a relationship with Justin would be. At any time he could end it. How long would it last? A few more nights? A week? A month or two? Until fate intervened?

Torn by this uncertainty, she questioned why she was clinging to him when there was no future? Why prolong the agony of a final good-bye? *Because you love him,* her heart answered. *You can't fight your love for him. How could anyone fight love?*

They finally reached the lake house. Justin was silent while opening the door, letting her enter. He followed, closing the door behind them. Wordlessly, they stared at each other. He then began undoing the buttons on his jacket.

"Go on and get ready for bed, sweetheart. I'll turn off the lights and lock up for you," he whispered softly.

Justin got detained when he had to return a call to one of his patients. When he finally appeared at the bedroom door, Lorren was curled up in the middle of the bed asleep. She was wearing a white satin sleep shirt, delicately designed with lace at the neck. She looked sensuous, but at the same time, innocent.

Justin walked over to the bed and stood gazing down at her. He shook his head. How could any man in his right mind not appreciate her? Only a fool would put her through what she'd suffered in her marriage. No woman deserved that. Especially not her.

A fierce surge of protectiveness, so intense it made Justin's legs shake, swept over him. He stepped away from the bed and began removing his clothes. He ached with the need to have her in his arms, and to hold her against him all through the night. He knew she still had a lot of inner healing to do, and he wanted to be there for her. He wanted to put more laugh lines in her face, and more joy and pleasure in her voice.

Climbing into bed beside her, he pulled her soft body to him. Sliding his arms around her waist, he buried his face in the curve of her neck.

Moments later, he joined her in sleep.

"Who'd ever have thought I'd actually enjoy spending time with my nose stuck in a decorating book?" Lorren asked herself.

Sitting on a kitchen stool and leaning over the breakfast counter, she paged through the huge catalog of fabrics Justin had given her nearly two weeks ago. A catalog of carpet samples lay tossed on the floor nearby.

She'd finally narrowed down the carpet selections to five colors she really liked. Now, if she could find colors for the draperies to complement her selections, she'd be pleased with herself.

She would be meeting Justin in town for lunch and wanted to advise him of her choices. And later, when he arrived home, she'd show them to him. She planned to meet with the interior designer again later in the week.

The past weeks had been absolutely wonderful. She and Justin spent most of their time together. In the afternoons, she worked on her writing, and he worked on finishing the charting of his patients. Then at night, they worked on each other. Waking up every morning in each other's arms, as the first rays of sunshine came through the bedroom window, had quickly become the norm.

Lorren smiled. There was no doubt in her mind that Justin Madaris was an extraordinary man. Not only was he successful in a profession he loved—the healing of the human body—he was also a man gifted in the art of healing the soul.

Her soul.

She'd come home to Ennis with barriers erected, an understandable means of protection after her marriage to Scott. No one, not even Syneda or Mama Nora, knew the emotional stress, the mental anguish she had battled. But like a beam of light, Justin had come into her life and gone about changing that. Like a fierce and mighty African warrior, he'd not only made her battle his, but with a sharp, pointed spear in hand, he had taken on the demons that haunted her.

Justin had done so many things. Simple things. Things like holding her hand whenever they went places together. Asking her opinions on various topics. Complimenting her often on her dress and looks.

They were simple things that Scott had never bothered doing. He'd said putting fanciful ideas in her head wasn't good, and he didn't believe in public displays of affection of any kind.

Then there were the special things Justin did. Things like holding her in his arms a long while after they made love. The sharing of his thoughts, his needs, his feelings with her. His ability to boost her spirits after she'd had a long, tiring, and unproductive day at writing.

Lorren couldn't help but think about the gifts he'd given to her for no reason at all—stuffed animals, flowers, candy—and then there were the candlelight dinners he prepared occasionally.

Simple things. Special things. All of them had meant so much to her. And all of them had shown her how much he cared. But still, she continued to be cautious in their relationship. She refused to let herself put too much stock in Justin's solicitous actions. Although there was no doubt in her mind that he cared, he still hadn't given her any reason to believe that she was the woman he loved and wanted to marry and have his children with. As far as she was concerned, he was still waiting for Ms. Fate.

The loud, piercing ringing of the telephone interrupted her thoughts.

"Hello?"

"Ms. Jacobs? This is Sandra Dickerson, Dr. Madaris's receptionist."

"Yes, Ms. Dickerson?"

"Dr. Madaris asked me to call and let you know he won't be able to meet you for lunch. It seems we have a little virus going around town and our office is swamped with patients. However, he hopes to leave here by four and was wondering if you could meet him at his ranch around five?"

"Sure," Lorren replied. "That won't be a problem." In fact, she thought, it would be perfect. Then she could go over the selections she'd narrowed down.

"Dr. Madaris left a key for you on the ledge above the front door."

"Okay. Thanks for calling, Ms. Dickerson." Lorren heard the click on the other end. But she continued to hold the phone in her hand, deep in thought. If Justin would be skipping lunch, he'd probably be starving by the time he met her at Taylor Oaks. An idea came into her mind. She would prepare something special to take to him when they met later.

Lorren cast her eyes on the massive ranch-style structure before her, and the tranquil beauty of the surrounding land of Taylor Oaks. No matter how often she came to this place, the view had always been simply breathtaking and had always held her spellbound.

Her favorite aspect of the house was its air of openness and warmth. Nearly every room overlooked a large enclosed patio, which featured a one-of-a-kind swimming pool. The pool had an unusual zigzag shape that was emphasized at night with some sort of special lights the Taylors had had installed. She remembered how the lights' soft glow subtly illuminated the patio and pool area after dark. It was a unique change from the harsh glare created by many other types of traditional pool lights.

She glanced around, not seeing Justin's car anywhere. Retrieving the key from its hiding place, she opened the door and entered the house. Her insides twisted in knots, knowing Justin would one day share this house with the woman he loved.

The foyer was completely empty. Only one rug adorned the floor. Moving farther inside she found the other rooms just as bare. She glanced around the living room. Justin would pay a pretty penny to completely refurnish this place, she thought, as the resinous smell of fresh paint teased her nostrils.

She visualized how she would decorate the house if it were hers. The house consisted of a huge living room, an enormous dining room, a spacious kitchen with bright countertops, a massive family room with a fireplace, an ample-size study, six bedrooms, a master suite with a fireplace, and five bathrooms.

The kitchen would have bright-colored appliances to accent its countertops. Except for the kitchen's polished tile floor, she would let the remaining floors of the house retain their dark oak. She wouldn't dare cover them up with carpet as Justin had suggested doing.

Along with the rustic walls, the oak floors bestowed upon the dwelling a bit of Western flare. Mrs. Taylor had told her all of the oak wood used throughout the house had come from the numerous oak trees that had been chopped down to clear way for the house.

On impulse Lorren walked into the spacious kitchen. Outside the kitchen window a particularly large oak tree provided shade for the kitchen and a couple of the bedrooms. Its lower limbs dipped and curved, nearly touching the ground. She remembered climbing that tree on a dare many years ago. It had been quite an experience, one that had gotten her a scolding from Mama Nora when she'd returned home with a soiled and torn skirt.

She placed the picnic basket on the long kitchen counter. It was at that point she heard the sound of shoes clicking loudly on the wooden floors.

"Lorren? Where are you?"

"In here."

Justin came into the kitchen. The sight of Lorren caused his heart to race and his entire body to react. Her hair hung ın a single French braid. He wanted to loosen it and let her hair fall unhindered about her shoulders.

She wore a pair of jeans that hugged her thighs and bottom enticingly. He could barely refrain from staring at her. She was staggeringly beautiful. He smiled. "Come here, Lorren." His voice was low and deep.

Lorren returned the smile, tilting her head to one side. "Pardon me, Doctor Madaris. I don't recall hearing you say please."

Justin watched as she pretended to dismiss him and went about the task of spreading a blanket on the kitchen floor. She grabbed the picnic basket he noticed for the first time. Leaning against the counter, he watched her empty the basket of its contents.

A platter of different cheeses, a bowl of salad, two large apples, a container of fried chicken, a small basket of grapes, rolls, a handful of napkins, some plastic utensils, wineglasses, and, last but not least, a bottle of wine, chilled California Chablis. He watched as she sat cross-legged on the blanket, her eyes shining, a bright smile on her luscious mouth. "The spread awaits you, sir."

Justin took a few steps and stood towering over her. He reached down and unceremoniously pulled her up into his arms and carried her to the counter. He set her down atop it.

"This," he murmured, "is what I want now. Food can wait a moment. This is what I've been starving for all day." He gently covered her mouth with his,

his tongue stroking her lips to grant him deeper penetration. She willingly parted her lips.

Once inside her mouth, his tongue tangled with hers. His hands caressed her back, and he gently pulled her closer, feeling a gnawing ache in his loins. He'd thought about savoring the taste of her tongue in his mouth all day. He tore his mouth from hers.

"I needed that," he said huskily, pulling in quick intakes of air. "Now we can eat."

He gathered her in his arms and carried her back to the blanket. Placing her on it, he joined her. They ate in silence. He watched her every movement; how she bit into a big apple and the way her mouth widened to cover it; how she devoured the cheeses slowly, one at a time, as if savoring each slice; the grapes, and how she licked her lips after each one.

But it was her eating of the chicken that pushed him over the edge. He watched as she again licked her lips before biting into a chicken leg, taking little nibble bites before taking a miniature plug out of it…then a little bigger plug…then another…

"That does it!"

Lorren's eyes widened when a half-eaten chicken leg was abruptly snatched from her. She was suddenly pulled into Justin's strong arms. "What's wrong with you?"

"Like you don't know," he muttered, stalking out of the room with her in his arms. "I've warned you about tempting me."

"I didn't tempt you." She laughed.

"Oh, yeah, you did. You had me actually envying your food, Lorren." He gently placed her on the lone rug in the foyer, staring down at her with an intensity that made a passionate chill flow down her spine. One look at the huge bulge pushing against his metal zipper said it all.

A sensuous grin appeared on Justin's face as he began unbuckling his belt. "We do *this* first, then we'll eat."

A smile touched the corners of Lorren's lips. "Fine with me. I wasn't all that hungry anyway. At least not for food."

The sound of Justin scrambling about on the floor beside her woke Lorren. He was naked on his hands and knees, searching for something.

Lorren couldn't believe she'd actually fallen asleep on the floor in the foyer not wearing a stitch of clothing. Her hair was no longer in a neat French braid, but hung in disarray around her shoulders. *Hell's bells! What if one of the workers had returned unexpectedly and walked in on them!* "Justin, what on earth are you looking for?"

He glanced at her. "Sorry. I didn't mean to wake you."

Lorren sat up. A grin touched her lips. "I can't believe I actually fell asleep after we, uh, you know." Her eyes wandered over Justin's body. The sight of him naked on all fours sent her blood racing. She cleared her throat. "So, what are you looking for?"

"My medallion. I seem to have lost it around here someplace. I know I had it on when I brought you in here."

"It'll turn up. Come on, let's go back in the kitchen and finish eating. I'm starving. You should be hungry yourself after that workout you just had." She stood and began dressing. "After we eat, I'll help you look for it."

Justin continued on with his purpose, ignoring her offer to help later. "Naw, I can look for it myself. I don't intend to leave until I've found it."

Lorren snapped her jeans. Her hands stilled at the waistband as she considered Justin's words. There was an urgency in his voice she'd never heard before.

"Justin, what's so special about the medallion? I noticed you wear it all the time. Is it some sort of fraternity memento from college?"

He looked up at her. "It was a gift. Denise gave it to me on our wedding night."

Lorren felt as though she'd been slapped. *He was frantically searching for something he'd received from his dead wife...and just moments after they'd made love!* "Oh, I see. Then by all means I hope you find it," she snapped, before turning and walking off toward the kitchen.

"Lorren, what's wrong with you? Come back here."

Justin stood. Quickly pulling on his pants, he followed her. By the time he caught up with her, she was on her knees repacking the basket.

"What's the matter with you, woman?"

She stood and faced him. "You got some nerve asking me that."

"Forgive me if I seem a little dense here, but I don't know what you're upset about."

"Then by all means, let me spell it out for you, Dr. Madaris. What's bothering me is the fact you've never mentioned the significance of the medallion."

Justin frowned. "And just what was I supposed to tell you? Have I ever asked for an accounting of every piece of jewelry you own? I really don't understand what the big deal is here."

"The big deal is you're still wearing a keepsake given to you by your wife, who's been dead ten years. As far as I'm concerned, wearing that medallion is no different from you wearing your wedding ring."

"For crying out loud. Why are you making such a big deal out of this?"

"Because any woman you become involved with has to compete against your wife's ghost, or what you perceive as the perfect memory, the perfect love." *Which is exactly what I've been doing without even realizing it.* "Whoever told you there's always tomorrow evidently forgot to tell you to let go of yesterday. And Justin Madaris, you haven't done that."

Grabbing her purse from the counter, she walked toward the door. Before reaching it, she turned back and gave him the same parting words he'd often given to her.

"Think about it."

Lorren walked out the door. She was nearly to her car when she heard Justin call her name. Ignoring him, she kept walking. Opening the car door, she slid inside, started the ignition, and drove off. Tears dimmed her vision. She wiped them away from her eyes.

With agonizing slowness, she recalled touching the medallion once or twice, and how Justin's body had stiffened in response to her contact. At the time she'd been too caught up in what they were doing to really think much about it. Now she did, and the thought made her cringe—even from the grave, Denise held Justin's heart captive.

When Lorren reached the lake house, she went inside and sank into the softness of the sofa. Her heart ached, and she was unable to control her tears any longer.

Justin continued to stare in the direction Lorren's car had taken, even when it was no longer in sight.

"Let her go," he angrily told himself, going back into the house and slamming the door closed behind him. "I don't need this," he muttered, pacing the floor between the kitchen and the foyer, looking for his medallion. "I should never have gotten involved with the woman. She's…she's…"

He stopped talking to himself, unable to complete the sentence. When he did moments later, the words echoed loudly in the room. "She's the first woman to bring some real happiness into my life since Denise."

Justin took a deep breath and slumped against the wall. He was stunned at the confusing feelings he was experiencing. Lorren couldn't be more wrong in what she'd said. He had let go of yesterday. But he could see why she thought he hadn't. He had to talk to her and make her understand.

He turned to leave and his gaze caught sight of the medallion on the floor near his feet. He reached down and picked it up. Several emotions passed over him while he looked at it—love, joy, pain… and fear. The first three emotions had been for Denise. The last one, for Lorren.

He was suddenly afraid that she had just walked out of his life.

Lorren jumped when she heard the sound of the doorbell. She stood. Her muscles were stiff and cramped. Glancing at her watch, she saw an hour had passed since she'd come home. She'd been sitting on the sofa all that time. Walking to the door, she opened it.

Justin stood in the doorway with the picnic basket in his hand. "May I come in so we can talk?"

Lorren drew in a shaky breath. She'd known she was going to have to see him sooner or later, but a part of her wished it could be later. Much later.

She wasn't sure if she was ready to hear whatever it was he wanted to say right now. He looked tense and exhausted, and his voice sounded ragged. She relented.

"Yes, come in," she replied, trying to keep her voice neutral, but knowing she'd failed miserably. She took a step backward and Justin entered the house, closing the door behind him.

Lorren walked across the room and sat in the wing chair. After placing the basket on the table, Justin stood with his back to her, gazing out the window at the lake. It seemed he stood that way for hours instead of minutes. When he finally turned around, his eyes were glazed with remembered pain. He stared at her, studying her, before he began speaking.

"It seems I'd known Denise forever, when actually we first met in high school. Her parents moved to Houston from Dallas in our sophomore year. Even then, I knew there was something special about her. We dated through high school and decided to wait until we'd finished college before marrying. She got a scholarship to Spelman in Atlanta, and I attended Howard."

There was a pause before he continued. "During the time we were apart, we were miserable. One day I couldn't take it any longer and purchased a plane ticket to Atlanta. When I got there, I asked her to marry me. Since there's no waiting period in Georgia, we got married that same day. Our parents, though surprised, were very supportive. Denise completed her semester at Spelman, then transferred to Howard to be with me. We got a small apartment near campus. It was hard at first, but we had each other and plenty of love."

Justin took a deep breath. "She'd finished college and was working at an accounting firm when her headaches began. At first we thought they were the result of stress. She'd been doing a lot of heavy studying for an upcoming CPA exam. But when she began having dizzy spells, we became alarmed and had her checked by a doctor. A CAT scan revealed an inoperable turmor at the base of her brain, and she was given less than six months to live."

Lorren watched the man she loved in the grip of emotional pain, reliving his tortured memories. A part of her wanted to put her arms around him and comfort him. However, she didn't move. She sat still while he continued.

"For us it was a lifetime of happiness and dreams to be snuffed out in less than six months." Justin paused suddenly, sucking in a deep gulp of air.

"Toward the end, she wanted to talk about my life without her, but I couldn't. For the first time in my life, I felt completely helpless. With all my medical knowledge, I could do nothing to prevent the inevitable. I felt like I had failed her somehow. I even began questioning whether I wanted to continue in the medical field. But Denise refused to let me blame myself and give up. She said life was too short for regrets."

He cleared his throat. "Although I knew the cold, hard facts surrounding her condition, a part of me kept hoping, kept praying. Deep down she understood what I was going through. The only thing she asked was that her last breath not be taken in the sterilized confines of a hospital. She wanted to be at home with me. During her final days, her body had weakened from the chemo treatment, but she maintained her good spirits until the end. We spent our days and nights together—alone. We wanted it that way, and, thankfully, our families understood."

The sound of Justin's voice became more hoarse. "She died one night while I held her in my arms. With the very last of her strength, she clutched my medallion and held it in the palm of her hand."

Lorren felt heartsick. The pain he'd endured watching the woman he loved die must have been devastating for him. Just like her parents' death had been to her. Fighting back tears, she stared at him and saw misty, pained eyes staring back into hers.

"Losing Denise," he continued, "was the hardest thing I've ever gone through. We shared so much. And I feel I lost so much."

He sighed deeply and walked over to the chair and knelt in front of Lorren, gripping her hand. "Whether or not I wear the medallion won't change the fact that I respond to you in ways I've never responded to any woman, including Denise. I never thought the void left in my life after her death would be filled. But you're doing it, Lorren. I just can't make any promises about anything right now."

New tears welled in Lorren's eyes as she tried to hold back her emotions. After hearing his story, her love for him gave her the strength to accept things as they were for now, and pray one day a change would come. She knew there was a chance he would never love her. There was a very strong possibility that the only woman he would ever be capable of loving had died ten years ago.

"Thanks for sharing that with me, Justin. It explains a lot of things."

He stood and nervously rubbed the palm of his hand over the back of his neck. "So, where do we go from here?"

A wry smile touched Lorren's lips. She wanted things back the way they'd been between them, and he was letting it be her decision. "Why don't we finish eating. I'm starved."

Justin stared down at her. His expression was one of heartfelt relief and thanks. A smile curled the corners of his mouth. "Me, too."

Lorren's gaze traveled over his handsome features and saw the sparkle had returned to his eyes. She stood. "So, did you find your medallion?"

He hesitated before answering. "Yes, I found it."

"Where is it?"

"Here." He touched his pants pocket.

She took a step toward him and reached into his pocket, pulling out the medallion. Accepting the reason why it was so special to him, she stood on tiptoe and placed it around his neck. "Now it's back where it belongs until you decide differently."

Justin grabbed her wrist. "You don't have to do this. If you prefer that I not—"

"No, it's okay. I'm fine now."

"Are you sure?"

"Yes, I'm sure." *I'm doing the right thing,* she told herself. *The decision to stop wearing it has to be his.*

When Justin gently pulled her into his arms, she reminded herself she was nothing more to him than the woman he enjoyed sharing his passion with, the woman who was helping him decorate the house he'd ultimately share with someone else.

And unknown to him, she was also the woman who loved him.

Chapter 10

"You better have a darn good reason for pulling me over," Justin said to the tall, handsome man wearing a huge grin on his face and a badge of the law on the blue shirt covering his broad chest.

"I believe I do," the man answered lazily, leaning down and resting both elbows in the car's open window. A wan shaft of sun struck his hair and it gleamed like dark gold. His grin broadened and his ocean blue eyes shone mischievously. "I have a deep appreciation for beautiful women, and the one sitting next to you looks too stunning for words."

"You haven't changed a bit, Roderick Clark," Lorren said, laughing. "You're still quite a character. Becoming sheriff hasn't changed you at all."

"Sure it has. Now I'm giving the tickets to speeders instead of getting them all myself. The reason I stopped you guys is because of Rhonda. That wife of mine sent me on a mission. She ordered me to find you, Lorren, and invite you over for dinner Friday night. We were out of town the night of Ms. Nora's birthday party and missed Justin's cookout because of Rod, Jr.'s little league game. Rhonda is determined for the two of you to get together so she can bring you up to date on the latest gossip in Ennis Place," he said jokingly. "It'll be a small gathering of a few couples." Then, seemingly as an afterthought, he added, "I guess that invitation also extends to you, Justin," he teased.

Lorren smiled. "That sounds like a great idea. I'd love seeing Rhonda again." She turned to Justin. "Is Friday night okay with you?"

"Sure. I wouldn't miss the chance to sample some of Rhonda's peach cobbler."

Rod raised a brow at his friend. "What makes you so sure she's making peach cobbler that night?"

Justin laughed. "Your wife wouldn't miss the chance to serve her prizewinning cobbler. I'm depending on you to keep her in a good mood till Friday. You know how testy pregnant women can get at times."

"Rhonda's pregnant?" Lorren asked, breaking into the men's conversation.

Rod beamed proudly. "Yep. She's pregnant with child number four, and the doctors have already said it's a boy." He checked his watch. "I'd better get going. I'll see you guys Friday night around seven."

"All right, Rod," Justin answered. "See you then."

The sound of loud music and laughter could be heard as Justin and Lorren walked up the sidewalk to the Clarks' home. Numerous cars were parked in the driveway.

"I thought Rod said this was to be a small gathering with a few couples," Lorren whispered to Justin when they reached the front door.

Justin chuckled. "If you know Rhonda well enough, you should know her small gatherings often get out of hand, especially where the number of people are concerned. She loves people and, because of it, she loves to entertain," he said, pressing the doorbell. "I met Rod a few years ago, when he worked with John a short while as a Texas Ranger, before becoming sheriff. A couple of weeks after I arrived in town, Rhonda invited me to dinner. She failed to tell me that half of Ennis would also be there. Her small dinner party turned into a full-scale welcome-to-town affair."

Amusement lurked in Lorren's eyes. "Remind me to tell you about the time Rhonda gave an all-girls party one night. You won't believe how it turned out."

Before Justin could ask for the details, the door opened and they found themselves greeted with hugs from a very pregnant woman.

"Lorren! Justin! I'm glad you made it," she said, pulling them into the house.

Justin and Lorren had been right. This was no small party. As Lorren looked around she eyed all the other guests. Some of them she recognized, and some she did not. A good number of them were crowded around a table laden with food.

"Let me take a look at you, Lorren Jacobs. I can't believe it. You haven't changed a bit. I bet you can still fit into your cheerleading outfit."

Lorren laughed. "Don't count on it. But what about you, busy lady? Three kids and a fourth on the way," she exclaimed with an I-don't-believe-it look. "What happened to your plans after high school to take Hollywood by storm?" Rhonda Clark was indeed a beauty, Lorren thought. She was a Jennifer Aniston look-alike and appeared even more radiant pregnant.

"What happened is a man by the name of Rod Clark. Surely you remember him," she teased. "I don't think anyone who has ever lived in Ennis could forget him. He's the guy who used to ride that Harley-Davidson motorcycle and wear that black leather jacket. He's also the guy all the mothers used to warn their daughters about."

She laughed. "Well, somehow he managed to put a ring on my finger and an even bigger one in my nose. The next thing I know, my plans of becoming an actress were history. What I do now, in between babies, is teach drama at the University of Texas in Dallas."

"It's about time the two of you got here," a loud male voice boomed from behind them. Wearing a huge grin, Rod walked up to greet the latest arrivals. He leaned down and gave Lorren a peck on the cheek and Justin a warm handshake. "I was just about to send my deputy out to find you."

He turned to his wife. "And what's this nonsense about mothers trying to keep their daughters from me?" He pulled her into his arms. "If that's true, your mom didn't do such a good job, did she, honey?" he drawled lovingly.

Rhonda giggled. "See what I mean, Lorren. I'm putty in this man's hands."

Love clearly shone in both of their eyes, Lorren thought, looking at the two individuals. She was touched by their warm, open display of affection.

"If the two of you are going to get mushy, Lorren and I will leave." Justin grinned.

"Why, Justin. We never get mushy." Rhonda laughed "Come on, let's pah-tay."

The four of them were still laughing when they were joined by the other guests. After quick introductions to the people Lorren didn't know, Rhonda proceeded to be the perfect hostess. Lorren was also introduced to the Clark clan. The two boys were clones of their father, and the little girl looked just like her mother. Lorren thought it was cute that all the family members' names began with "R." Rod and Rhonda's daughter's name was Rochelle, and their sons were Rod, Jr., and Randle.

An hour or so later, Lorren and Justin found themselves in the kitchen, escaping the crowd. They were enjoying the party but decided to sneak away for a moment of privacy. Justin had just reached out to take Lorren into his arms when the kitchen door flew open and Rhonda walked in.

"Not in my kitchen, you don't. Now who's getting mushy?" she teased, opening the refrigerator to take out another tray of food.

"Where's Rod?" Justin asked.

"He's somewhere out in the backyard showing David Myers his skill at gardening. He has a little vegetable garden on the other side of the house away from the pool."

"Rod's growing a garden? This I gotta see." Justin gave Lorren a quick kiss on the lips before going out the back door in search of his friend.

"I think I'd better open the windows," Rhonda said jokingly. "I don't know if I can stand the heat the two of you generate."

Lorren almost choked on the punch she was sipping.

"Don't you dare get embarrassed, Lorren Jacobs," Rhonda said sternly. "You're in the home of friends. Besides, you and Justin deserve to be happy. Everyone knows he's a widower, and news about your divorce got around pretty fast. I think the two of you getting together is pretty neat."

"But it isn't what you think. Justin and I are just friends," Lorren protested.

"Wow! Some kind of friendship," Rhonda said as her eyes lit up. "It hasn't slipped by me that this is the first time Justin's let you out of his sight all night, and I bet he'll be back in here before you know it."

No sooner had the words been spoken than Justin reentered the kitchen. Lorren met Rhonda's teasing I-told-you-so eyes from across the room before their laughter broke to the surface.

Justin looked at them both curiously. "What's so funny?"

"It's a private joke, Justin," Rhonda said teasingly, wiping the tears coursing down her cheeks.

"That could be dangerous, knowing the two of you."

Rhonda grinned. "Relax, Doc. We're completely harmless."

Justin extended his hand to Lorren. "Let's rejoin the party."

"All right." Lorren enjoyed being around him. His presence was like a safety net and she felt thoroughly entwined in it.

When they rejoined the others, she couldn't help noticing they were the object of a lot of people's curious stares. Although Justin joined in the conversations around them, he never once left her side for long. And when he did, she was always within range of his watchful eyes.

"Enjoying the party, baby?" he asked, when they found themselves alone on the patio overlooking the pool.

"Yes. What about you?"

Justin stared at her for a moment. "I'm having a blast, but wish I was someplace else right now," he said softly.

Lorren was entranced by his chocolate-colored eyes. "Oh? Where?"

"Your bed."

A soft gasp escaped her with his words. There was a tingling in the pit of her stomach. "I wish you were someplace else, too," she whispered, her heart fluttering wildly in her breast.

Justin's gaze was soft as a caress. "Where?"

"Deep inside of me."

For a long moment neither of them spoke. They gazed into each other's eyes, their breathing becoming heavy.

Justin's words broke their silence. "Shall we find Rod and Rhonda and tell them good-night?"

Lorren nodded. "Yes. That's a good idea."

Later that night, Lorren sat in the dark watching Justin. From the way he was breathing, it was evident he was very deep in sleep. He hadn't even stirred when she'd left the bed.

She pulled the spread around her naked shoulders to guard against the late-night chill that crept through the room. Leaning back in the chair, she felt moisture gathering in her eyes.

"You're a very special man, Justin Madaris," she whispered softly. In his own unique way, using what he'd often referred to as tender, loving care, he had helped her overcome the sexual inhibitions that had been deeply rooted inside of her. Thanks to his patience, understanding, and tender, loving nature, she no longer felt panicky whenever she recognized her body's need for him, those tremulous sensations within her that were still new and unfamiliar. Like the ones she'd experienced tonight at the party that had made her bold enough to say what she'd said to him.

Justin had repeatedly shown her that the driving, physical longings she felt were a natural, normal, and healthy reaction to the attraction between them. Yet at the same time, he had unknowingly proved that her desire for him wasn't the only thing she felt. Her love grew stronger each day.

Lorren knew in her heart she had never known or truly loved a man until him.

Main Street was lined with people eagerly waiting for the parade to begin. Each year, on the first weekend in May, the township of Ennis and its neighboring counties came together for a jam-packed weekend of laughter and fun, highlighting the National Polka Festival. The festivities began Saturday morning with a giant parade. It was a sunny morning with hordes of people and children.

Justin and Lorren were dressed in shorts and festive T-shirts commemorating the event, and had conveniently found a shady spot under a huge oak tree, providing them a good view of the coming procession.

With a camera firmly in her hand, Lorren began snapping pictures as the gaiety and excitement made her relive some of her most cherished memories of living in Ennis.

Participants in costumes, bands from various schools, and floats from numerous organizations dazzled the spectators. A giggle of excitement bubbled up in Lorren's throat when the float from the Children's Home Society came by.

"Look, Justin!"

"I see it, baby," he answered. "That's a nice-looking float. The kids really did an outstanding job putting it together."

Lorren twisted her head to smile at him, not realizing because of the crowd, they were standing so close. Another inch and their lips would have made contact. Not giving in to the temptation, she simply turned her head back to watch the float. The feel of Justin's arms around her waist tightened and sent her a message that he understood.

"Later," he whispered for her ears only.

After the parade, they wound their way through the crowds of people. They walked hand in hand, darting along paths, around babies in strollers, and stopped at various booths to try out a variety of treats.

"I want some popcorn, Justin," Lorren said, pointing to a nearby vendor.

Justin dug a bill from the back pocket of his

shorts. "For a woman who usually doesn't eat much, you're costing me a bundle today," he teased. "What do I get in return?"

"Are you being obnoxious?" she asked, as a grin tilted her lips.

Reaching across her to share some of the popcorn, he whispered in her ear, "I refuse to answer that. Just wait until I get you home, lady. For punishment, I'm going to make love to you over and over again."

Lorren slid her gaze to his. "Promises, promises."

They came to a group that was watching boys and girls perform precision gymnastics routines. She leaned back against Justin, letting her head rest intimately on his chest.

"What time is it?" she asked silkily, raising her eyes to his.

Justin checked his watch. "Almost three. The Festival dance starts at four. Do you want to hang around until then?"

"No."

"Where would you like to go?"

Lorren shrugged sheepishly. "Pat's Bookstore."

He lifted a brow. "The bookstore? Why?"

Lorren smiled. "My books are arriving today."

Justin returned her smile. "Then by all means, let's go check them out, Ms. Famous Author." They began walking hand in hand away from the crowd.

"Dr. Madaris! Yoo-hoo, Dr. Madaris!"

They turned to the short, bald man racing toward them. "Hello, Mr. Coleman," Justin greeted.

"Hello," he replied, and acknowledged Lorren with a nod when Justin made the introductions. "I was wondering if I could ask you a couple of questions about the medicine you mentioned that would work wonders for my back pain. You don't mind if I borrow him for a few minutes, Ms. Jacobs?"

"No, not at all. I'll just browse through that little shop over there," Lorren replied, giving Justin a smile of understanding.

He pulled her to him and brushed her lips with his, not caring they had an audience. "Don't go far."

Lorren entered the art shop, which was adorned with many gift ideas. She was staring at some beautiful ebony art figurines that she thought would be perfect to add to Justin's collection when a man's deep voice spoke from behind.

"Hello, Lorren. It's been a while. How have you been?"

She whirled around, recognizing that voice anywhere. It belonged to the man who had caused her so much heartache, shame, and misery. He was the one man she had never wanted to see again. The shock on her face extended to her eyes.

"Scott! What are you doing here?" Standing just under six feet tall, he stood smiling down at her as if they were the best of old friends. He had lost a few pounds since she'd seen him last but, other than that, he looked the same. She used to think he was a handsome man. And there was no doubt in her mind that some women would still think so. His golden-colored eyes, strong jaw, and the cleft in his chin were features most would consider striking. But those were things people saw on the outside. On the inside, he had everything it took to make up a sleazy human being.

"I was hoping I'd run into you."

Anger flared in Lorren's eyes. "Why?"

"So we could talk."

"There's nothing we have to say to each other, Scott. We said it all the day of our divorce." Bitterness laced her every word. How could she have ever thought she loved him? How could she have ever thought at one time he was special? And how could she have tolerated the pain he'd caused her for two years?

She sighed deeply. How many times during her marriage had she gone to sleep crying from his cruel words? And how many times had he apologized for his ill use of her, and she'd forgiven him?

"Baby, surely you don't mean that."

Lorren flinched at the endearment and threw her words at him like stones. "I mean every word. We have nothing to say to each other. Good-bye."

He was silent for a long moment and she could tell he was controlling his anger. He was known to have a quick temper when things weren't going his way.

"All right, Lorren. Now isn't a good time to talk. You're upset, I can see that, and it's understandable. I treated you badly while we were married, and I regret it. I've missed you, baby."

She laughed in his face. "Missed me? Give me a break, Scott."

His smile faded. "I've given you more than a break, Lorren. I've given you a year. Don't forget we still have some of the same friends. And according to what I've been hearing, you haven't been doing a whole lot of dating since our divorce. And that can only mean one thing. You haven't gotten over me. What other possible reason could you have for moving back to this dreary little town?"

Lorren was speechless at Scott's incorrect assumptions.

"I'm willing to take you back, baby," he continued, as if he had walked out on her instead of it being the other way around. "I'll even agree to go with you to counseling sessions for that little problem of yours. This time, we'll work things out together. But like I said, now isn't a good time to talk. I'm going to hang around town for a few days. When I think you're ready to see me, I'll give you a call. See ya."

Lorren watched as he turned and walked out of the shop, becoming lost in the crowd. She was still too stunned to speak. Of all the nerve! Scott Howard had just proved beyond a shadow of a doubt that he was a conceited jerk. And it only made her feel just that much more ashamed of how stupid she'd been to have ever gotten involved with him.

"See anything you like?"

Lorren turned when she heard Justin's voice. He slid his arms around her waist.

"Lorren, what's wrong? You're shaking."

She inhaled deeply. Should she mention seeing Scott to Justin? No. There really was no need. Contrary to what Scott thought, she wasn't pining away for him. She was free of him, and he couldn't hurt or humiliate her anymore. And if he did try contacting her as he claimed he would do, she would refuse to talk to him.

"Lorren?"

Bringing her thoughts back to the present, she met Justin's concerned gaze. "I'm fine, Justin. And no, I didn't see anything I liked. Besides"—she forced a smile—"as you reminded me earlier, I've spent enough of your money for one day."

Justin grinned. "Go ahead, woman, and break me. I'm enjoying every minute of it. Are you ready to go to the bookstore?"

Her smile widened. "Yes, let's go."

Chapter 11

There was a slight breeze coming in off the lake, and the scent of bluebonnets was heavy in the air. Dusk crept through the trees and surrounded the land in a purple mist.

Justin and Lorren stood on the porch and watched as night came. Its arrival beckoned the moon and stars to show their faces.

Lorren's arm was around Justin's waist as she nestled her head against the broad expanse of his chest. She was unusually quiet, and had been since they had returned home from the Festival.

"Lorren?"

"Ummm?"

"A penny for your thoughts."

Lorren shifted slightly. *You're better off not knowing them.* She felt Justin's cheek resting on top of her head. His arms felt warm and strong as they caressed her back.

She turned her head slightly and looked up at him. There was no way she could tell him that she'd been trying to convince herself that she really hadn't seen Scott in Ennis that afternoon; and that she really hadn't talked to him.

But the truth of the matter was she had, and she couldn't help but remember his words... *"When I think you're ready to see me, I'll give you a call...."*

Lorren turned back to look at the lake and decided not to share with Justin her present thoughts, but to share with him some of her earlier ones.

"I was just thinking how wonderful this day has been and how I hate to see it come to an end."

She felt Justin smile against her temple. "Do you know what my favorite part of the day was?" he asked.

She laughed softly, giving her head a nod. "I think I have an idea, but tell me anyway."

"Our visit to the bookstore." He laughed as he pulled her closer to him. "It's nice to know a celebrity."

Lorren's mood lightened with Justin's teasing. When they had reached the bookstore, she'd discovered she wasn't the only person who had anxiously awaited the arrival of her books. The store had been swarming with a crowd of children and their parents, who wanted to purchase the newest Kente Kids book.

She soon found herself surrounded by the children, who wanted her to autograph their books. Justin had found the scene rather amusing and had waited patiently, something Scott would never have done, while she accommodated each and every child. He didn't like kids—something he hadn't bothered to mention until after they'd gotten married. Besides, Scott had always been slightly jealous of her work.

Justin, on the other hand, seemed immensely proud of her. He'd even taken the time to keep some of the smaller children occupied by gathering them in a group and reading some scenes out of her book to them. He had kept them entranced with the words that flowed from his mouth. His deep voice made the characters in her book come to life, and the African names rolled easily off his tongue.

She had been so rapt as she watched him thumb through the pages, reading to the children. He truly loved kids, and it showed. She could envision a little boy with Justin's strong features, and a little girl with her daddy's heartwarming smile.

Lorren noticed some of the parents had also gotten caught up in Justin's recitation. He was so compelling, his magnetism was so rich. His vitality completely captivated everyone around him.

She tipped her head back to look at him. She was driven to ask the one question that amazed her about him ever since he'd told her about his wife's death. "How did you do it, Justin? How were you able to bounce back after suffering so much pain?"

For a long moment he didn't say anything, and for a while she thought he was not going to answer. He was overcome with emotion when he finally spoke. It was evident his composure was under attack.

"I'd be a liar if I said it was easy. Because it wasn't. But somehow, at some point in time, you learn not to let the pain destroy you, and not let the hurt haunt you every waking moment. You have to believe it'll go away eventually…if you let it. But," he went on, "not before you ask yourself a thousand times, why me? What did I do to deserve such heartache, such misery, such pain?"

He took a deep breath before continuing. "Pretty soon you get tired of looking for answers that won't come. You finally make up your mind to leave behind the thing you can't change—your past, and concentrate on the thing that you can—your future."

Lorren wished she could have taken that attitude when she'd become engulfed in her pain. She had gotten so wrapped up in the hurt, she hadn't been able to see beyond it. Even now she hurt when she remembered how things had been between her and Scott, and the lies he'd told.

She wondered how long it would take before her pain completely faded. At what point would she stop looking for answers to questions regarding Scott's treatment of her? One thing was for sure, she thought, as a smile tugged at the corner of her mouth. Justin had become the best pain reliever around.

"While I have you exactly where I want you, Lorren, there's something I'd like to ask you."

"What?"

"I'm going home to Houston in a few days. My parents are giving my baby sister a sweet sixteen party. The entire family will be there, and I'd like you to go with me."

Lorren twisted in his arms so that she could see his face. She didn't want to read more into his invitation than was really there. But a part of her couldn't stop the happiness that flowed through her. "Will it be okay with your parents if I were to come?"

"Sure. My parents, especially my mother, will be ecstatic. She's dying to meet you."

"In that case, I can't disappoint her, can I?"

Justin laughed. "No, you can't. And believe me, you won't."

Later that night Lorren sat at her desk, working on an outline for a new book. The ringing of the telephone interrupted her thoughts.

"Hello?"

No one answered her, although she heard a deep, breathing sound on the other end.

"Hello?" she repeated.

A quiet click sounded in her ear when the caller hung up on her.

Lorren took a deep breath. Common sense told her the caller evidently had gotten a wrong number, or it had been a bored teenager with nothing else to do on a Saturday night but play games on the telephone.

But another part of her, the one that dealt more with caution than common sense, couldn't help wondering if…

"Was that a wrong number, Lorren?"

Lorren looked up. Justin had completed his shower and stood in the doorway of the bedroom with the towel wrapped around his waist. His upper body gleamed a golden brown in the soft light, and the beads of water on his shoulder shimmered like jewels.

There was a tremor in her voice when she answered. "Yes, apparently." She found it difficult to draw air past the heaviness unfolding in her chest.

"Are you coming to bed now?" he asked huskily, walking toward her, his gaze never leaving hers.

All thoughts of completing the outline for her book were lost. "Yes, I think I will."

Justin gathered her into his embrace. "Good. I'd be lonely in bed without you."

Lorren rested her cheek against his damp chest, feeling his strength and the very essence of him. His iron-muscled thighs felt warm against the soft cotton of her shorts. All thoughts of the phone call left her mind.

She stepped back out of his arms. Without taking her eyes off his, she began removing her clothes. "The last thing I want is for you to be lonely."

Lorren lifted her eyelids slowly, trying to ignore the sunlight dancing along the windowsill and sliding into her room. She didn't want to wake up just yet.

"Uhmmm," she moaned, closing her eyes again. The memories she encountered when shutting them made the very air around her seem electrified. All during the night and the early morning hours, Justin had loved her.

Their bodies had come together with the reverence of intense hunger and the promise of total fulfillment. And it had continued until Justin had received an emergency call and left.

The warmth of the bedroom as well as the clock on her bedside table told Lorren it was well into the morning. Eleven o'clock to be exact.

She was about to get out of bed when the telephone rang. Thinking it could possibly be Justin or Mama Nora, she quickly picked it up.

"Hello?"

"Are you in a better mood to talk to me, sweetheart?"

Lorren's shoulders stiffened and her fingers tightened their grip on the phone. "Why are you calling, Scott? I've told you, we have nothing to say to each other."

"But we do. I want us to get back together. Baby, I admit I was wrong and want to make it up to you. Just give me a—"

Lorren pushed the button, disconnecting the call. She placed the phone back on the receiver, not wanting to hear anything he had to say.

The telephone rang again. She flinched at the sound. She refused to answer the phone. There was no way she would believe Scott wanted a reconciliation with her. There had to be another reason for his sudden interest after a year.

She would bet any amount of money that he'd heard about her pending business deal with Corvel Toy Company. If everything worked out, that deal would become a very profitable venture. Scott was a big enough jerk to try to woo her back just to be able to cash in on her success.

The phone stopped ringing and Lorren took a deep breath and tried to relax. She got out of bed and started for the bathroom. She stopped in the doorway when the phone began ringing once again. Biting her lips, she entered the bathroom and closed the door, shutting off the shrill tone of the ringing phone.

"Why didn't you answer the phone?"

Lorren spun around from the kitchen counter at the sound of the welcome voice. Her gaze traveling the length of him, Lorren thought just how good Justin looked dressed in a pair of jeans and a pullover shirt. "What?"

He walked over and hugged her, then held her away. "I asked why you didn't answer the phone, baby. I tried calling you a couple of times from the hospital."

"Oh. I may have been in the shower, or I may have been outside," she replied half-truthfully. "What did you want?"

Justin pulled her back into his arms. "I thought

I'd let you know that I ran into Rod at the hospital, and he told me Rhonda delivered last night. They have another son."

Lorren glanced up, happiness for their friends shining in her eyes. "Oh, Justin, that's wonderful. Give me all the details."

Justin laughed. "Of course Rod says the kid looks just like him. He weighed nine pounds and twelve ounces. Both mom and baby are doing fine. Rod claims his newest son will be ready to play for the Cowboys in twenty-two years." Justin shook his head. "Poor kid. Who would want to play for the Cowboys?"

Lorren flashed him a piqued look. "Watch it, Justin. You're really asking for trouble." She grinned. "What are they going to name him? I'm sure whatever it is, it'll begin with the letter 'R.'"

"They're naming him Royce."

"Royce? I like that," Lorren replied, nodding. "It's a pretty name."

"Wrong."

Lorren raised a brow. "Wrong?"

"Yes, wrong. Boys names aren't pretty. Girls names are."

Lorren smiled. "That sounds a little chauvinistic, but I guess I really can't expect much better from a Texans' fan."

Justin laughed, then placed a kiss on her lips. "How would you like to go out to dinner, then drop by the hospital to see Rhonda and the baby?"

Lorren's smile widened. She needed to get away from the house for a while to get her muddled thoughts together. "I'd really like that."

It was nearly seven in the evening when Justin and Lorren returned. Dusk was just beginning to settle in.

"Sandra cleared my calendar for tomorrow, and I was wondering if you wanted to leave for Houston earlier than we'd planned?" Justin asked as they entered Lorren's house.

"That'll be fine," Lorren replied. She was anxious to get away for a while. All during dinner, her nerves had been stretched to the limits, not knowing if Scott was still hanging around. She didn't want to run into him again. Hopefully, while she was out of town, he would give up his insane idea of their talking and return to California.

"Let's dance, Lorren."

"What?" She looked up at Justin, a bit confused.

"I said let's dance."

Lorren's ears suddenly picked up the soft sound of Toni Braxton as it floated through the room. Justin must have turned on her CD player while her thoughts had been a million miles away.

"Sure," she said, going into his outstretched arms. He pulled her closer to him, and she drew comfort from his hard body as they slowly swayed to the music.

Lorren knew in reality that Justin wasn't actually dancing. What he was doing was holding her so that every inch of her body felt every hard inch of his. Evidently he'd sensed something was bothering her, and, in his own special way, he was giving her a portion of his inner strength.

Resting his cheek against the top of her head, he swayed gently from side to side, holding her close. His arms tightened around her.

"What's bothering you, baby?" Justin murmured against her ear. "I'm a good listener if you want to talk about it."

Lorren took a deep breath. He was giving her the perfect opportunity to open up to him, to tell him about Scott's calls. Deep down she wanted to, but to confide in him about it also meant telling him about the last night she'd spent with Scott. She'd told no one about that night, not even Syneda, although Lorren was sure Syneda had an idea of what might have happened to make her finally leave Scott.

She shuddered with shame each time she thought of how naive she'd been. Would Justin understand anyone being that stupid and gullible? His marriage had been perfect, free of blemishes. Would he comprehend the nature of a troubled marriage?

Because of her uncertainties, she couldn't bring herself to talk about Scott to him. At least not yet.

She raised her head to look up at him and decided to talk about something else that had been on her mind. "I'm a little nervous about meeting your family."

He grinned down at her. "Don't be. They'll love you."

Lorren smiled. "You think so?"

"Baby, I know so. Trust me."

Justin pulled his Corvette to a stop in front of the spacious, two-story house. Coming around to the passenger side of the car, he opened the door for Lorren, linking his arms through hers. "We'll get the bags later." He bent down, brushing his lips to hers. "Still a little nervous?"

She grinned. "Should I be?"

"It depends on how brave you are. There're fourteen of us, counting spouses and nephews. We can be a pretty rowdy bunch when we all get together. You've already met Clayton, and he's the worst one of all."

Lorren laughed. "I found your brother to be very charming."

Justin chuckled. "Don't let the charming act fool you, honey. Clayton is a smooth operator," he said, ringing the doorbell.

The front door opened and a pretty teenage girl with dark eyes, toasted almond skin, and vibrant reddish brown hair stood in its frame.

"Justin!" she squealed, throwing her arms around him.

Justin returned the hug. "This is the birthday

girl," he said to Lorren, drawing her inside the house. "Lorren, I'd like you to meet my baby sister, Christina Marie Madaris, but we call her Christy."

"Hi," the girl smiled, offering Lorren her hand in a friendly handshake.

Lorren returned the smile. "Hi, and happy birthday."

"Thanks." Christy then turned to Justin. "Where's my birthday present?"

"The girl has no tact."

Lorren's head whipped around at the deep masculine voice. Leaning against a wall was a tall handsome man with charcoal gray eyes, dark wavy hair, and nut-brown skin. His sculptured mouth curved into a smile as he straightened his stance and came toward them.

"Blame it on Clayton," Justin jokingly replied, giving the man a hearty bear hug. "Christy convinced Mom and Dad to let her go live with Clayton a few weeks last summer while the folks were vacationing in Florida. Would you believe I haven't been able to de-Claytonize her since?"

Justin turned to Lorren. "My brother Dex." To Dex he said, "I'd like you to meet Lorren Jacobs."

Lorren found her hand resting in the man's firm grip. His eyes bored into hers assessingly. "You wouldn't happen to have any sisters, would you?"

Lorren laughed. "No. I was an only child."

Dex chuckled. "Too bad."

"But she has a close friend who most assuredly

has got it goin' on," a third masculine voice intruded. Lorren turned and gave Clayton Madaris a smile as he entered the foyer to join them. Like the other two Madaris men, he was devastatingly handsome. He had dark hair, soft sable skin, and brown eyes the exact color of Justin's.

"I'm disappointed you didn't bring Syneda with you," Clayton said.

Justin lifted eyes heavenward. "I'm sure you'll get over it. Where there's a woman concerned, you usually do."

Clayton chuckled. "I don't know about that, bro. It's not too often I meet a gorgeous woman who enjoys discussing Roe versus Wade as much as I do."

Justin grinned. "It sounded as though the two of you were debating the case more than discussing it."

Clayton smiled, shaking hands with his brother. "We did seem to have a little difference of opinion." His smile widened as he turned to the woman at his brother's side.

"Lorren, it's good to see you again. I'm glad you could make it. You'll bring beauty and warmth to our dreary family gathering as we come together to celebrate the birthday of the milkman's kid."

Justin and Dex laughed at his statement. "I think you've lost me," Lorren replied, smiling. She gazed from one brother to another, totally confused.

"Don't mind them, Lorren," Christy said, coming to her aid. "My brothers have this thing about me being the milkman's kid since I have reddish hair.

The truth of the matter is our paternal great-grandmother also had natural reddish brown hair, so I inherited my hair coloring from her."

Clayton laughed throatily. "Christy's been telling people that story for years. I know for a fact our great-grandmother's hair was just as black as mine."

"Cut it out, Clayton," Dex admonished playfully. "We don't want to upset the birthday girl too much. Did anyone tell big brother that little sister is going out on her first date tonight?"

Before Justin could open his mouth Christy rushed in. "The rest of the family is waiting for us in the den. They can't wait to meet you, Lorren."

Justin put his arm around Lorren's shoulders as they began to walk down the hall. "What do you think so far?"

Lorren laughed. "Like you said earlier, you're a rowdy group, but so far I feel right at home."

Moments later Lorren felt even more at home. She was overwhelmed by the friendliness of Justin's family. His father, a larger model of Justin, gave her a hug as if she wasn't a stranger but a family member. His mother, an elegant-looking, petite woman, with dark hair and charcoal gray eyes, smiled with genuine delight at meeting her. Now Lorren knew where Dex had inherited his eye color.

"It's nice to finally meet you," Marilyn Madaris said. Her warm smile and welcoming gaze put Lorren completely at ease. "I'm glad Justin brought you home with him."

"Thanks for having me," Lorren replied. "It's a pleasure to meet you, too. And you have such a lovely home."

Justin's other two sisters, Kattie and Traci, were very attractive and friendly. They pulled her from their big brother's side the minute they were all introduced. Their handsome husbands gave her smiles and warm hellos.

Lorren was even more surprised to learn she had a fan club of two with Justin's older nephews, both seven, who told her they'd read all her Kente Kids books and asked for her autograph. The little boys said they couldn't wait to go back to school and tell everyone that Lorren Jacobs, the writer and creator of the Kente Kids, was their Uncle Justin's girlfriend.

Lorren smiled, knowing this was the beginning of a glorious weekend.

The three Madaris brothers sat around the table playing cards. Their parents and Lorren had retired hours ago.

"Lorren's a nice girl, Justin."

Justin smiled, pulling another card off the deck. "Thanks, Dex. I have to agree with you."

"Is there something we should know, Big Brother?" Dex asked, as a smile touched his lips. "If my memory serves me correctly, you've never brought a lady friend home for us to meet since Denise died. Although I've been in Australia for two years, I'm sure I would have heard about it through the family grapevine if you had. Is there some meaning in this?"

Justin met his brother's gaze. "She's special."

"We guessed that much, Justin. How about telling us something we don't know," Clayton said, throwing a card out.

Justin shrugged. "There's nothing to tell. She's just special."

A huge grin covered Clayton's face. "Special as in marriage?"

Justin gave him a hard glare. "Special as in special, Clayton. Don't read more into it than that. Lorren's been married before, and the experience wasn't good. She's been left with a deep scar."

"I know exactly how that can be," Dex said drily.

Justin looked long and steady at his brother, who sat studying his hand. "Dex, have you tried contacting Caitlin since you've been back in the States?"

Dex's head snapped up sharply. His eyes locked with his older brother's. They stared at each other for a tense moment. Complete understanding flowed between the three men at the table. They were not only linked together by blood, but also by deep concern and love for each other.

"No, I haven't, and I don't intend to either. Caitlin made it very clear that our marriage was over. I've accepted that."

Justin nodded. "All right," he replied, not missing

the anguish he heard in his brother's words. Then a smile touched his lips. "Since we've discussed my love life and yours, I guess it's time to discuss Clayton's. Has anyone told you about the woman he was dating last winter?"

Dex shook his head. "No. What about her?"

"Don't you dare remind me about that woman, Justin," Clayton bellowed.

Justin laughed. "I thought she was rather a nice girl. I especially thought she had a nice set of teeth."

Dex raised a brow. "Then what was the problem?"

Clayton answered, smiling. "Her nice set of teeth was the problem. She got turned on from biting her dates. She was a regular Miss Vampire. At first her bites seemed harmless enough, a little nibble here and a little nibble there. Then suddenly her nibbles became full-fledged bites. I had the good fortune of having her teeth print on my rear end for at least a month. Talk about a very sore behind."

Roaring laughter engulfed the table, and the card game was momentarily forgotten.

Dex shook his head. "It seems, kid brother, you still have a penchant for the unusual."

That night Lorren had trouble sleeping. She and Justin had been given separate rooms, which made her acutely aware of how long it had been since she'd slept alone. They had been sharing a bed continuously since the night of the storm over a month ago.

The evening had been full of fun and excitement. Justin had been right. He had a warm, loving family who did get a little rambunctious at times. A smile quirked her lips as she remembered the hard time the three brothers had given Christy's date, Michael. One would have thought the Madaris brothers worked for the FBI with the interrogation they'd put him through.

Once Michael had been introduced to everyone, the three brothers had huddled him off in a corner. Lorren only hoped Christy had warned Michael beforehand what to expect from her brothers. She hadn't seemed the least annoyed or upset with their behavior. Evidently she was used to their high degree of overprotectiveness.

Michael, on the other hand, was a nervous wreck when the brothers all but read him his rights, with Clayton using legal jargon, Justin using medical terms, and Dex using no terms at all but giving the young man bold eye contact.

The Madaris clan had dined at a restaurant where a section had been reserved just for them. After dinner the family surprised Christy when the owner of the establishment, along with a few of the waiters, had sung happy birthday to her and brought out a lovely cake adorned with sixteen candles. After cake and ice cream had been served and adequately eaten by all, Christy and Michael stood to leave. They'd made plans earlier to join friends for a movie.

"Don't forget our discussion, Michael," Clayton

said easily, not bothering to lower his voice. "Remember what I told you about justifiable homicides."

"And don't forget what I told you about how many bones there are in the human body, and how painful it feels if any of them are broken," Justin added pointedly.

Lorren looked at Dex to see what friendly reminder he would offer Michael. Evidently the other family members had the same inclination, for all eyes turned to him. He gave them a lazy smile, then said to Michael in a voice that was deep and deadly, "One wrong move, kid, and I'll personally boil you in oil."

After dinner the rest of them had returned to the Madarises' home. The men played a friendly game of cards, the kids retired to the family room to watch a Disney movie, and the women sat around discussing changing trends in fashion, movies, and assorted other topics of feminine interest.

Lorren had thoroughly enjoyed their company. More than once she'd looked up to find Justin's eyes on her.

The house was quiet. Justin's sisters and their families had left for their own homes, and she and Justin's parents had gone to bed shortly thereafter, leaving Justin, Dex, and Clayton up playing cards as they waited for Christy's return from her date.

Tomorrow would be another day full of activities. Justin's sisters and his mother had invited her to go shopping with them. Afterward, she and Justin would leave to return to Ennis.

She took a deep breath. Why had Justin brought her here? She had turned that question over in her mind since he'd issued the invitation. One of his sisters had mentioned that Justin had not brought a woman home for them to meet since his wife's death. Lorren could only hope he was considering a meaningful, long-term, committed relationship with her. She didn't know how much longer she could deal with not knowing how long their relationship would last.

She couldn't help wondering when Ms. Fate arrived, where that would leave her.

Why did he bring Lorren here?

The question plagued Justin. His mind replayed all the scenes that had taken place since he and Lorren had arrived. Just as he knew they would be, his family was completely taken with her. And every chance they got, they made sure he knew it.

And he wasn't sure just how he felt about that.

He was beginning to get annoyed with his family's hints that "It's about time" and "She's the girl." They couldn't seem to understand that his life wasn't being governed by the ticking of some internal biological clock. He still wanted the usual things in life. He wanted to remarry, have a bunch of kids, and watch them grow while living on the ranch he'd bought.

Years ago he'd chosen to leave his future to fate.

And although he enjoyed his relationship with Lorren, he had no reason to believe she was the woman he'd been waiting for.

For starters, she didn't believe in love and marriage. She'd said so the night they met. And although he knew she'd been spending a lot of time with Vincent ever since the camping trip, he didn't really know how she felt about having kids of her own someday.

Besides those things, she hadn't given him any reason to believe she would put down her roots in Ennis permanently. For all he knew, she'd only moved back to lick her wounds.

Then there was the main reason that stood out. She was totally different from Denise in a number of ways, especially one in particular. Denise had always been soft and gentle, and he'd always treated her that way, even while they made love.

Lorren, on the other hand, wouldn't accept gentleness. She could fuel a want and need in him until he took her with a force that stunned him. Even now, he had to grind his teeth to hold back a deep, rough groan threatening to escape him just from thinking about her.

"Couldn't you sleep?"

Justin turned from staring out the kitchen window. His mother's question had invaded his thoughts. "I should be asking you the same thing."

Marilyn Madaris smiled. "I wish I could go to sleep, but your father's snoring tonight is worse than ever. It must be from the excitement of having all of his children home," she said, unhooking two coffee cups from the cup rack and filling them with the coffee Justin had made. She handed him a cup. "Oh, by the way, Justin. I think Lorren's a lovely girl."

He took a sip of coffee. "So what else is new?"

Marilyn Madaris stared at him. "Why are you getting upset? Don't you think she's a lovely girl?"

"Of course I do. I just don't want the family reading more into my relationship with Lorren than what's really there."

"Then you tell us, Justin. How should we read this? She's the first woman you've brought home since Denise died."

"But that doesn't necessarily mean she'll be the last. That's all I'm saying, Mom. I like Lorren. I like her a lot. We enjoy each other's company but..."

Marilyn Madaris raised a brow. "But what?"

"Nothing." He set his cup of coffee on the counter. "Good night, Mom."

Marilyn Madaris watched her oldest son walk out of the kitchen. It was her guess that his "song singing days" were coming to an end. She couldn't help but wonder how he would handle it when that fact hit him?

Justin slid into bed after doing one hundred push-ups and just as many jumping jacks. He really hadn't expected to get much sleep, especially since he wasn't sharing a bed with the one person he wanted to sleep with.

His mother had put Lorren down the hall in one of his sister's old rooms, and the thought that she was so close yet so far irritated him. He tossed and turned most of the night.

He arose at the crack of dawn and went downstairs for coffee and was surprised to find Clayton and Dex already up, drinking coffee and eating toast. Clayton was the first to speak.

"What in the world was happening in your room last night, Justin?"

Confused, Justin raised a brow as he poured himself a cup of coffee. "Nothing that I know of."

Clayton grinned. "Then that explains why you were making all that racket working off your frustrations. Leave it to dear old Mom to put Lorren in the bedroom next to theirs, out of your reach."

Clayton plopped the last piece of toast in his mouth and washed it down with coffee before adding, "Whatever it is you're afflicted with, you got it bad, Big Brother. And I hope it's not contagious."

Justin shot Clayton a dark look. He refused to ask him what he meant by that comment. He then threw a thunderous gaze in Dex's direction.

"Don't look at me, Justin," Dex said, grinning. "I haven't said a word."

"Good. And see that you don't."

Justin was still in a testy mood when the rest of the family came down for breakfast a little while later. He found himself staring at Lorren as she made her way around the kitchen, helping his mother prepare breakfast. The sight of her dressed in something simple, like a denim wrap skirt and peasant blouse, made his entire body ache. His hands felt damp and a film of perspiration began forming on his upper lip.

And to make matters worse, he found his two brothers watching him and grinning from ear to ear. They didn't seem the least bit threatened when he shot them a murderous look.

That afternoon didn't come fast enough for Justin. Although he had enjoyed the time he'd spent with his family, he was more than ready to leave. Bidding them farewell, he loaded both the luggage and Lorren into the car in record time and headed back to Ennis.

He kept a firm grip on the steering wheel and fought the temptation to reach out and run his hand over Lorren.

He took a deep steadying breath. They couldn't get back to Ennis quick enough to suit him.

Chapter 12

"Aren't we going to bring in our bags?"

"Later," Justin muttered, guiding Lorren through the door and locking it firmly behind them. He didn't waste any time pulling her into his arms. "Do you have any idea how much I want you? How much I need you?"

Not as much as I want you to want and need me, Lorren thought, seeing the heavy look of male hunger in his eyes.

Justin kissed her, and she arched herself against him, forgetting everything except the touch of his lips, the taste of his mouth, and the feel of his hands moving over her body.

In one smooth motion he picked her up in his

arms and carried her to the bedroom. Lorren felt the heat of his gaze touch every part of her skin as he undressed her.

Then he quickly removed his own clothes and took time to prepare himself for her, to keep her safe.

Wordlessly, they stared at each other. She wanted to tell him she loved him, but knew she couldn't. Instead, when his mouth met hers again, she kissed him with all the longing in her heart.

Lorren put into action what she dared not say in words. Letting her love for him be a guide, she gave to him a passion the likes of which she'd never before given, wrapping him in the sensuous warmth of her feelings. She became bold, she became daring, she became a tormentor, and, in the end, she became a pleaser. She would always remember the exact moment their bodies became one, fitting together perfectly.

Closing her eyes against the surge of fierce pleasure clutching her, she urged him deeper into her, absorbing the tremors of rapture that flowed through her body.

"Lorren!" Justin breathed her name sharply in her ear at the same time he drove them both over the edge.

Lorren woke early the next morning, sprawled across Justin's chest and securely cradled in his embrace.

Last night they had made love with a hungry intensity she'd never imagined possible. It was as if they couldn't get enough of each other. His body had claimed her as fire bolts of desire raced through her.

Her body had understood his rhythm and, instinctively, arched to meet his steady thrusts of possession. The fires burning between them had somehow gotten out of control, becoming a fiery blaze of ecstasy. After their hunger had been temporarily satisfied, they'd slept, then wakened and made love again and again.

Justin stirred slightly. Lorren slowly eased off him, not wanting to wake him. "Where're you going?" he murmured, pulling her back firmly against him.

An easy smile played at the corners of Lorren's mouth. "To make coffee and get something to eat. We sort of skipped dinner yesterday."

Her eyes glowed with playfulness as she continued. "So let me go, Justin Madaris, or suffer the consequences. You know how testy I get whenever I'm hungry."

Lorren felt the pressure of his hands loosen some. "All right, baby. I'll let you go, but only if you promise you'll come back."

She smiled down at him, marveling at the handsome features looking back at her. His dark eyes were soft with slumber. She took his face in her hands and kissed his lips. "I promise."

He released her completely then and, when she stood, rolled onto his stomach and buried his head in the pillow.

Lorren took slow steps to the bathroom. The tenderness in her thighs and deep in her body reminded her of the strength of Justin and the intensity of their lovemaking.

After taking a shower and changing into a pair of shorts and a T-shirt, she went into the kitchen and put on a pot of coffee. Opening the pantry, she took out a box of cereal and opened the refrigerator for the milk when the phone rang.

She answered it absently. "Hello."

"Where have you been the last couple of days, Lorren? I needed to talk to you."

Lorren immediately recognized the voice, and her body stiffened as rage engulfed her. "You just wait one minute. I don't owe you an explanation about anything. I don't want to talk to you, and if you call here again, I'll notify the police. There are laws against harassment. Do you hear me?"

The only response Lorren received was a click in her ear. She placed the phone back in the cradle and leaned against the counter to catch her breath, fighting to control her shaking body.

"Do you want to tell me what the hell is going on?"

Lorren whirled around to find Justin leaning against the kitchen door. He was completely awake now, and he wasn't smiling.

When she didn't answer him, he walked over to her and put his hands on her shoulders, gently squeezing. "Who was that on the phone, Lorren?"

Somehow she found herself leaning against him,

absorbing the strength that was an innate part of him. "It was Scott."

Justin muttered a soft curse. The arms that surrounded her stiffened. "What did he want?"

"He wants to talk."

His mouth tightened. "Has he called you here before?"

Lorren nodded. "Yes. He's called a few times since the day I saw him—"

"Saw him?" Justin asked, easing her away from him, cutting off her words. "You saw him? Here in Ennis?"

"Yes."

"When?"

Her voice was quiet. "At the Polka Festival last week."

Justin exhaled through clenched teeth. "Why didn't you say something?"

She cast her eyes downward. "Because I didn't want to bother you. It was my problem."

Justin lifted her chin with his finger so their eyes could meet. "Baby, your problems are my problems. Don't you know that?"

"No, and it really doesn't matter. I've brought enough emotional garbage into this relationship without adding more."

"Emotional garbage? What are you talking about? You had a bad first marriage, but you're not the first and certainly won't be the last. There are problems in every marriage."

A part of Lorren didn't want Justin's tenderness and understanding at the moment. It was the part of her that couldn't forgive herself for being a fool and staying with Scott as long as she did. That part of her wanted to lash out, and, unfortunately, Justin was the target.

Her eyes flashed with fire when she looked at him. "What do you know about problems in a marriage? Yours was perfect. You got the person you wanted and the two of you would have lived happily-ever-after had she not died."

Lorren's eyes filled with tears as she continued. "You don't have any idea how it feels to believe you've chosen the perfect mate, and then have that person turn on you and try to destroy your self-respect and dignity. You can't begin to imagine how it feels when your inability to pleasure him in bed becomes something he belittles you with, day and night."

Justin reached out. She moved a few inches away from him. "No, you can't imagine any of those things, Justin, because your marriage was perfect. It was made in heaven. All of us aren't that lucky."

The last thread of Lorren's composure crumbled, and she gave in to her tears. She was powerless to resist Justin when he picked her up in his arms and carried her to the living room, while she sobbed into his chest.

"That's right, baby. Get it all out. Let yourself cry. Get rid of the anger, the frustration, and the hurt. And after you've finished, I'll give you as much tender, loving care as anyone could possibly receive. I will make you feel loved, and I'll show you just how special you are."

"But you don't understand," she got out between sobs.

Justin sat on the sofa and cradled her in his lap. "Baby, I *do* understand. Nobody's marriage is perfect, and I'm sorry I gave you the impression that mine was. Denise and I disagreed about a number of things. But we didn't allow our disagreements to come between us."

He placed his lips against her cheek, kissing away the tears there. "You don't have to experience pain firsthand to understand it, Lorren. Someone I love and respect very much, my brother Dex, met and fell in love with Caitlin at a time when all of us thought he never would. He had promised himself years before that he would never give his heart to a woman after a close friend of his committed suicide after receiving a 'Dear John' letter."

Justin's thumb absently traced circular motions on Lorren's arm while he continued. "Greg and Dex were as close as brothers since the time they were kids. They attended Morehouse together. Greg met and fell in love with someone who attended a neighboring college."

Justin pulled Lorren closer. "To make a long story short, the girl broke things off. Dex was the one who found Greg when Dex went back to their apartment in between classes. Greg had shot himself in the head. He left Dex a note that said… 'Don't ever fall in love. It hurts like hell.'"

Lorren drew back, remaining absolutely motionless as she absorbed Justin's words. Her heart went out to the man who had taken his life on account of love. "But Dex eventually fell in love, didn't he?"

"Yes, nearly twelve years later. He met and fell in love with a younger woman, a lot younger. Caitlin was barely twenty-one and fresh out of college when Dex married her at thirty-two. They met when she came to work at my uncle's ranch for the summer. Dex and Caitlin fell in love immediately, and were married in less than two weeks. The company Dex worked for was sending him to Australia for two years."

Justin's hand slowly stroked her back. It was a soothing feeling. "Caitlin was to join Dex in Australia."

"Did she?"

"No. What she did was send him a 'Dear John' letter along with divorce papers and her wedding ring. None of us really knows the complete story, and Dex refuses to talk about it."

"It must have been awful for him."

"Yes, it was, and he still hasn't completely gotten over it. He was in a foreign country without his family and friends for support. He had to go through that painful period in his life alone."

Justin gave her a level look. "So you see, Lorren, I *do* understand the depth of your pain, just as I understand Dex's. You aren't the only person whose life was nearly destroyed by falling in love. Even I was hurt by love, but in a different way."

Lorren knew Justin was right and her anger began dissolving. She appreciated him for sharing Dex's story with her. It made her realize she wasn't in a class by herself. Pain hadn't singled her out for attack as she wanted to believe at times.

"Lorren?"

"Ummm?"

"What are you planning to do about your ex-husband?"

Lorren's eyes met Justin's, then glanced away. She wondered how much of her phone conversation with Scott he had overheard. "Hopefully, I won't have to do anything. I'm praying that he finally realizes I won't talk to him and leaves town."

"And if he doesn't?"

Lorren turned to face Justin again. She stirred uneasily at the thought of Scott remaining in Ennis, trying to persuade her to talk with him. "I really don't know, Justin. I'll probably talk to Rod to see what can be done to stop him from calling me. Legally, Scott is out of my life."

"Do you have any idea why he's here?"

"He claims he wants a reconciliation, but of course I don't believe that for one minute. It's my guess that he's found out about my possible deal with Corvel Toys and wants a piece of the action. I can't believe he thinks I'll be stupid enough to take him back. There's no way I'll ever do that."

Justin was quiet for a moment before he spoke. "There's more to it than what you're telling me, isn't there?"

She swallowed. "What do you mean?"

"What did he do to you to make you afraid of him? I can detect it in your voice."

She shrugged. "You know that already. He tried convincing me that as a woman I was worthless."

"No. I think there's more to it than that. What aren't you telling me, Lorren?"

She chewed on her lower lip as she looked at him. "What makes you think I'm not telling you something?"

"Just a hunch."

He saw the wary look in her eyes. "Knowing about the emotional abuse you endured while married to him, I can understand your anger at him for being in town. I can even understand your being furious at the thought that he's contacting you, wanting the two of you to get back together. But I can't understand your being afraid. Unless..."

"Unless what?" she asked uneasily.

Justin didn't reply for a long time. Lorren knew he was seriously considering what he was about to say. "Unless he was physically abusive to you as well. That would explain your fear."

Lorren looked away from Justin quickly. She

tried to move away. His hands tightened around her waist. When he spoke again, his voice was velvet edged with steel. "Was he, Lorren?"

"I'd rather not talk about it, Justin."

"Tell me. Did he hit you?"

Every fiber in Lorren's body shook with the anger she heard in Justin's voice and the hardened look in his features. He rested his hand lightly against her chin, his voice husky with tenderness when he said, "I have to know."

His touch acted like a catalyst that destroyed the last of the self-protective shield surrounding her. She loved him and wanted to share everything with him. Even if it was a part of her life she'd rather not remember.

"Yes. He hit me, but only once. That was the night I finally left him."

She wished she could expunge the memories of that night from her mind. "He'd been out with his friends, and I gather I'd been the topic of their conversation for the evening."

"He discussed your personal lives with his friends?" Justin asked, his voice incredulous with rage.

"I found out later that night that he had. They had given him advice on how to whip me into shape. And he came home and tried to do just that, literally. My only advantage was that Syneda had talked me into taking a self-defense course after there had been a series of rapes in the LA area. I effectively used the right maneuvers to defend myself from his attack and get away from him."

Her eyes were misty. "But he did manage to hit me a few times, since he'd caught me unawares. I'd been asleep when he'd come in. He jerked me out of bed and began whipping me with his belt. I got a few bloody cuts from the buckle and had to get medical attention."

Justin's eyes conveyed the fury within him. She tried ignoring it as she continued. "That night I saw a different side of Scott. It was a side I'll never forget. I knew then that, when pushed to the limit, he was capable of anything. That's why I don't want to talk to him."

Justin combed his fingers through Lorren's hair. A part of him wished it was her ex-husband's neck instead. "Why haven't you told me about this before?"

She drew a deep breath. "Because I felt ashamed at having let him do that to me, and for being naive enough to marry him in the first place. I should have known what he was capable of. I should not have given him the opportunity to make my life a living hell. But I did, all in the name of love."

Justin's eyes softened as he gazed into her tear-stained face. "You have no reason to be ashamed, Lorren. He is the one who should be ashamed of what he's put you through. Was last week the first time you've seen him since the divorce?"

"Yes."

He pulled her closer. "I think we should pay Rod a visit and make him aware of what's going on."

"All right." Lorren sighed, pressing closer to Justin. She hoped the phone calls would be reason enough for Rod to ask Scott to leave town.

"What do you mean he agreed to leave town voluntarily?"

Justin leaned against the desk with his arms folded across his chest as he waited for Rod to answer his question. A dark scowl covered his face.

He and Lorren had driven into town earlier that day and met with Rod. He'd sat and listened while Lorren had given Rod her account of the calls she'd gotten from her ex-husband. Afterward, they'd left to visit awhile with Ms. Nora. Then Justin had dropped Lorren off to visit Rhonda and the baby. He had returned to talk to Rod alone.

Rod eyed his friend. "Just what I said. He left town voluntarily. I didn't have to throw him out. After you and Lorren left, I paid the guy a visit. He was staying at Cullers Inn and was already packing to leave when I got there. Since we always have a number of strangers lingering around after the Festival, no one in town gave his presence much thought."

Rob took a sip of coffee. "He comes across as a likable guy. There doesn't appear to be a mean streak in his entire body. In fact, he appeared rather pleasant."

"A likeable guy? Pleasant? Hah! If you believe

that, I have some prime vacation land to sell you in Alaska."

Rod grinned. "I said he *seemed* to be a likable and pleasant guy, Justin. In this business, I discovered a long time ago people aren't always what they seem to be. Besides, I've known Lorren since grade school, and I have no reason not to believe her story about him."

Rod leaned back in his chair. "I talked with him for over half an hour. He said he came to Ennis to talk Lorren into giving him another chance. He hadn't intended for his phone calls to upset her. Since he now knows she's against the idea of the two of them getting back together, he's willing to leave her alone."

Justin arched a brow. "He actually told you all of that?"

"Yeah."

"Sounds like the two of you got rather chummy."

Rod chuckled. "Not hardly."

"Are you sure he's left town?" Justin asked.

"I gave him personal escort service into Dallas myself. I also told him that if he ever came back to Ennis and tried contacting Lorren, I'd arrest him."

Justin sighed as he fished in his pocket and pulled out his car keys. "I should have gone with you to see him."

"No, you did the right thing by letting me handle it, Justin. You're too close to the situation, too close to Lorren. Things could have gotten a little messy with you there." Rod's eyes sparkled teasingly. "I take that back. Things could have gotten a whole lot messy with you there. When you came into my office this morning with Lorren, you were out for blood. I had to talk you out of going looking for him yourself. You were like a lion out to protect his lioness—at any cost."

Justin met his friend's stare. "I don't want him to ever hurt her again, Rod."

"I understand that," Rod replied, tipping his head back to look up at Justin. He saw the anger flaring in Justin's eyes. He hoped, for Lorren's ex-husband's sake, the man had the good sense to stay away from Ennis and leave Lorren alone. Rod wasn't sure if Justin even realized it, but he was wearing his heart on his sleeve.

Rod stood. "Just to be on the safe side, I'm going to keep a close eye on things in town. And I plan to have one of my men cruise the area around Elliot Lake more often for a while, just to make sure Mr. Howard doesn't change his mind about revisiting Ennis."

"Thanks, Rod, I'd appreciate it."

"Tell Lorren if she receives any calls that sound even remotely suspicious to let me know."

Lorren placed the last of the dishes in the sink before turning around to Justin. "But I don't understand why Rod wants a police car cruising the area when Scott has left town."

"It's a safety measure in case he didn't quite understand he's not welcome in Ennis."

Lorren turned back to the sink. Reaching up, she opened the cabinet and placed a bowl inside. Justin's eyes were drawn to the soft material of her skirt as it clung to her bottom. When she lifted her arms, his gaze zeroed in on her fine hips and shapely thighs as the material stretched upward. His body immediately hardened.

"Don't do that, baby," he said huskily.

Lorren turned around and gave him a strange look. "Don't do what?"

"Don't reach up like that."

Their eyes held. Then Lorren's lips curved into a mischievous smile when understanding dawned. "Oh, you mean don't reach up like this?" she asked, deliberately reaching up farther this time.

"Woman, you're really asking for it," Justin said, his voice strained.

"Asking for what?"

"You know what," he muttered, getting out of his chair and walking toward her.

Lorren laughed when she saw the evidence of his desire straining against his jeans. "You always want me."

"Yes, I always want you," Justin agreed, placing his arms around her waist.

"That makes me feel good," she said, leaning into him. "For so long I considered myself undesirable."

Justin pulled her closer. "Oh, but you are desirable, baby. Too desirable for your own good," he said, as he began fumbling with the buttons on her blouse. "And mine."

Chapter 13

A week later, dressed in shorts and a knit top, Lorren leaned back from the papers spread across her desk. She had been up since sunrise, putting the finishing touches on her book, and hadn't eaten breakfast. A cup of coffee was all she'd had, and now her stomach was rebelling.

Glancing around the room, she felt Justin's absence. He'd gone into the office to work half a day and had invited her to join him for lunch at Sophie's Diner.

The tile floor felt cool under her bare feet as she walked into the kitchen. Even though it was still early, she had about two more hours of writing time left before joining Justin for lunch.

By eleven o'clock, she had completed her writing, showered and changed into a challis print skirt and silk blouse, and was ready to leave. She had just grabbed her car keys off the table when she heard the doorbell.

Lorren gasped when she looked through the peephole in the door to see who was on the other side.

Scott!

What was he doing back in Ennis after Rod had warned him against returning?

For a few moments, she stood with her hand on the doorknob, trying to decide what to do. She squared her shoulders when her internal fuming had reached the boiling point. She'd had enough of Scott.

Snatching open the door, she confronted the man who was standing before her dressed impeccably in a tailored suit. "What are you doing here, Scott?"

He reached into his jacket pocket and pulled out a small gift-wrapped box. "I bought you a gift. It's sort of a peace offering."

Lorren couldn't help remembering the other times he'd caused her pain, then brought her gifts to make up for it. In the past, she had fallen for such gestures. But not anymore.

"No thanks. I don't want it."

"You're really going to like this, Lorren," he continued, ignoring her remark. "It cost me a bundle, but you're worth every penny. I really should be angry with you for sending that small-town cop after me. But I know you're still upset about how things ended between us."

He held the gift out to her. “Take it, Lorren. I got it especially for you.”

Lorren’s eyes narrowed. “I don’t want it, Scott. Understand? Things are over between us.”

Scott hesitated, then stuffed the box back into his pocket. “I don’t believe that, and neither do you. You love me too much.”

The corners of his mouth curved upward. “Besides, what other man would put up with you and your problem, baby?”

“That does it!” Lorren tried slamming the door in his face, but Scott, suspecting what she was about to do, blocked its closing with his foot and pushed his way into the house.

“Forceful entry is against the law, Scott. You’re already in hot water for even being here. I would advise you to leave. Now!”

He shrugged his shoulder, walked into the center of the room, and glanced around. “Nice place, but it’s not where you belong. You belong back in California with me. There’s nothing for you here in this little depressing town.”

Lorren continued to stand by the open door, determined to keep distance between them. “I happen to disagree. Everything I’ve ever wanted is here.”

“You’re just not thinking clearly, sweetheart.” His voice softened cajolingly. “I know that while we were married I wasn’t the perfect husband, but I promise to do better. I even plan to help promote your career more. I’ve heard about your deal with

Corvel, but I've got even bigger plans for you. How does the idea of the Kente Kids going to television grab you?"

Scott leaned against the bookcase with his arms crossed, a satisfied grin on his face, and continued. "I've run the idea of the Kente Kids becoming a Saturday morning cartoon show past my boss, and he absolutely loves it. He believes they'd be a smash hit. Just think what that could mean. There haven't been all-black cartoons on television since Cosby's Fat Albert series. I can just see all the bucks rolling in, not to mention the recognition the network will give me as the creator of the series."

Lorren stared at him. It was hard to believe she hadn't seen through his self-centered, smooth-talking, scheming ways before they had married. But she hadn't. Would she ever be able to get over her faulty judgment in choosing him for a husband?

Anger, the likes of which she'd never known, ripped through her. She slowly left her place near the door and walked a little farther into the room.

"You've got it all worked out, haven't you?" Lorren asked, her voice as chilling as her expression.

Scott didn't pick up on it either. He smiled, obviously thinking Lorren was giving him a compliment. "Yes, baby. I do."

Lorren laughed. "Well, I hate to disappoint you, but you've evidently forgotten one major detail."

His smile faded. He raised a brow. "What?"

"Me, and how I would feel about your whole

scheme of things. I wouldn't take you back, Scott Howard, if you were the last man on earth. Thanks to God, you're not. And I certainly wouldn't let you manage my career. My agent is doing a remarkable job, and I have no complaints. In fact, another network has already made us a similar offer, which I'm seriously considering at the moment. So forget it, Scott. I'm not interested in you or your deals. So get out."

Something cold flashed in Scott's eyes. His lips drew back in a snarl and he took a step toward her. "You little—"

"Don't even think about touching her."

Scott halted, going instantly still at the sound of the low, lethal, masculine voice. His gaze flew to the man who stood just inside the doorway. "Just who the hell are you?"

Justin ignored Scott's question, and instead spoke to Lorren in a controlled voice. "Come here, baby."

Scott's eyes narrowed when Lorren didn't waste any time going into Justin's outstretched arms.

"You okay?" Justin asked her softly, placing his arms securely around her waist.

Lorren nodded. "Yes, I'm fine. But how did you know about—"

"The police cruiser. I was at Rod's office when one of his men radioed in that he had seen a rental car in the area, and that the driver fitted this man's description."

Scott, obviously unnerved by the sight of Lorren in Justin's embrace, spoke up. "Look you. I don't know who you are, but you can't just barge in here. This is between me and my wife."

Justin's eyes darkened, and Scott had the good sense to take a step back. "Don't ever refer to Lorren as your wife. She was, and still is, too good for you."

Scott laughed viciously and sneered. "Too good for me? Is that what you think about that cold, empty woman standing next to you? Boy are you in for a surprise. She's nothing but a beautiful shell."

Justin took a step forward. "Why you—"

"All right, that's enough!" A uniformed Rod Clark walked into the house. He first fastened his level gaze on Justin. "I'm going to give you a ticket for speeding, Justin. You were doing every bit of ninety in that Corvette getting here."

He then turned his attention to the other man. "And you, Mr. Howard, evidently don't understand simple English. I thought I made it clear just a few days ago that you weren't welcome in Ennis."

Scott's shoulder lifted in a dismissing shrug. "This is a free country, Sheriff, and I can go anywhere I please."

Rod squinted at the ceiling for a moment, then looked at Scott again. "Not in my town, and not when it involves harassing one of the citizens I'm duty bound to protect."

Rod turned to Lorren. "How do you want me to handle this? Just say the word and Mr. Howard will be my guest for a few days in the Ennis Park Suite Jail, cell number ten."

Lorren clasped her hands in front of her, squaring her shoulders. "He's leaving, Rod, and he's not coming back. I think Scott has finally realized there's nothing here in Ennis for him. And since he claims he came here on behalf of the network where he works, I'm sure the president of that company would not take too kindly to one of their up-and-coming junior executives behaving in such a despicable manner. I don't want to, but if I have to, I *will* cause trouble for him. I have both the means and the funds to do it now."

She turned to Scott. "Do you understand what I'm saying, Scott?"

He glared at her and the two men. "I understand."

"Then I would suggest that you get in your car, leave, and don't come back."

Scott threw them all one last disapproving glance, then strode through the doorway. Rod and Justin followed behind him.

He had made it to the porch and was just about to walk down the steps when he whispered sneeringly to Justin. "Man, you're making a big mistake if you're thinking about making her your woman. She ain't worth your effort in bed."

By the time Lorren reached the porch, she found Scott sprawled on his face in the front yard. "What happened?"

Justin shrugged. "He slipped."

"I did not," Scott yelled, pushing himself up on his elbows. "You tripped me."

"Your word against mine."

"Sheriff, you saw him," Scott said, getting to his feet and wiping dirt off his expensive suit. "He tripped me."

"Sorry, I didn't see a thing, Mr. Howard. The sun temporarily blinded me. Are you sure you weren't just a little clumsy?" Rod asked, grabbing Scott's arm and leading him over to the rental car.

"I'm going to waste the taxpayers' money one more time and escort you across the county line. If you come back again, causing problems, I'll make sure you find out just how mean I can be when my patience is tried."

Rod yanked open the driver's door to the rental car and shoved Scott inside. He then walked casually around the vehicle to his patrol car.

"Don't think I'm going to forget about that ticket, Justin," Rod said, before getting inside the vehicle.

"I didn't think for one minute that you would," Justin replied. He walked over to Scott's car to have a few words with him. He lowered his voice to a deadly tone.

"Just thought I'd tell you before you go, Howard, just in case you're thinking about returning—Lorren belongs to me. And what's mine I keep and protect. If you ever try contacting her again, you'll have me to deal with. Just remember that."

An angry Scott nodded before starting the engine and pulling away, with Rod following behind.

When the two vehicles could no longer be seen, Justin walked back up to the porch.

"You sure you're okay?"

Lorren nodded as Justin followed her back inside the house and closed the door behind them.

"Yes, I'm all right. Scott forced his way inside here and there was nothing I could do," she replied, kicking off her shoes and walking into the bedroom.

Justin followed.

Mindless of the fact that she'd just gotten dressed to meet Justin for lunch moments earlier, Lorren began stripping off her clothes and rehanging them neatly in the closet. She didn't want thoughts of Scott to consume her. He had been a big mistake in her life, but she had to accept that and move on. But he had taught her a very valuable lesson—all that glittered was not gold.

Lorren shuddered and forced herself to clear her mind. Right now she only wanted to concentrate on the man leaning against the bedroom door, watching her. He was the man she loved more than anything, and at this very moment she needed him to make her feel whole.

"You're one tough lady, Lorren Jacobs. I was proud of you today."

She frowned slightly, feeling somewhat undeserving of his words. "I was scared, Justin. But I couldn't let Scott know it. For once, I wanted to stand up to him."

"You did, and I really don't think you'll hear from him again."

"I hope not."

Lorren backed up a few steps until the back of her legs touched the side of the bed. "Love me, Justin," she whispered. "Please love me. Now."

Justin straightened his stance and walked toward the woman standing next to the bed, wearing a lacy black bra and a black half slip.

"We're missing lunch," he said huskily, coming to stand in front of her. "And we'll probably miss dinner, too."

Lorren framed his face with her hands, pulling him to her. "Right now, I have a totally different type of hunger. One only you can feed," she said, moments before his lips covered hers.

Beautiful.

The fragrance Lorren wore and the scent of their lovemaking combined forces and retriggered primitive yearnings deep within Justin. However, he refused to give in to the urge to make love to her again…at least, not yet.

It was late afternoon and dusk was slowly approaching. They had only been out of the bedroom once, and that had been when Rod had dropped by to deliver the speeding ticket.

He and Lorren had used that time to grab something to eat, only to return to the bedroom. Now she lay snuggled against him, asleep. Her soft curves molded to the contours of his body. He allowed his gaze to travel over her face.

Beautiful.

There was no other word he could think of that would describe not only her, but also what they had shared that afternoon. Their lovemaking had spiraled to new heights.

Some sort of desperation had driven both of them, had consumed them. It had made them so wild and out of control that the bed was a complete mess because of it. The bottom sheet had somehow worked its way to the top; pillows and the bedcover were strewn on the floor.

Justin breathed deeply. The truth of the matter was that, even with the hot, fiery turbulence of their mating, he had felt something beyond just satisfying their bodies. He'd felt an inner contentment he hadn't felt in a long time.

How had Lorren accomplished something in a couple of months that other women hadn't been able to achieve in ten years? How could she make him feel so complete? So whole?

He continued to hold her as his thoughts shifted to Denise. She had been his first love, and he appreciated that fact. Through her, he had been able to grow and mature.

He could now admit that after her death he had compared every woman he would meet to her and none would measure up. It hadn't dawned on him until much later that there was not another Denise Wakefield Madaris out there, and it wouldn't be fair to her memory to try to find one. Deep down he never thought he'd get lucky enough to find the kind of happiness he and Denise had shared a second time.

Then he'd met Lorren.

From the first moment he'd seen her that night, he had wanted her, needed her. With Lorren he was a different person, which proved that over the years he had changed in many ways. He couldn't help but wonder had Denise lived, if she would have been able to adjust to those changes.

He now admitted he'd reached an age where a totally different type of woman appealed to him. A woman glowing in the image of fire and passion. A woman capable of stimulating him physically as well as mentally.

A woman like Lorren.

He stroked the length of her back, holding her closer to his body, and even closer to his heart. It was an act of emotion-filled possession. An act of love.

The thought hit him full force. He loved Lorren. She was the woman of his fate.

And with that realization came something else, ice-cold fear. He was scared to death of loving someone again and losing her. He was frightened of experiencing more pain, and he wasn't sure he was ready to give up his heart again, so totally and completely.

Fear's icy grasp tightened. Loving was for a lifetime. Loving was forever. Love meant emotional vulnerability. He had discovered the hard way that there was pain in loving someone, and what he felt for Lorren was stronger and deeper than what he'd felt for Denise.

A conversation he'd had with his mother a few months ago filtered through his mind…

"I'd remarry in a heartbeat if the right woman came along, Mom, you know that," he chuckled.

"Do I, Justin? I'm beginning to think this fate song you've been singing over the years is for the birds. A part of me can't help but wonder if perhaps you're only fooling yourself."

"Fooling myself? About what?"

"About ever wanting to marry again…."

His mother had been right. He'd only been fooling himself.

He suddenly came face-to-face with the reality of the lie he'd been telling himself, his family, and everyone around him for the last ten years. Waiting on fate had just been an excuse not to get deeply involved with anyone, not to give up his heart.

And now he was faced with the hard fact that fate had done exactly what he'd claimed it would do. It had given him a woman he couldn't imagine living his life without. And that in itself was his greatest fear.

No! I can't handle this. I need time to think. I need time to work this out. I need time to make sure.

But still, even with all his uncertainties, he knew he had to be fair to Denise's memory and the love they'd once shared. Although Denise would always hold a special place in his heart, he loved Lorren now. Reaching up, he removed the medallion from around his neck. Being careful not to awaken Lorren, he opened the drawer to the nightstand next to the bed and placed it inside. Tomorrow he would take it home and put it in the small trunk where he kept his other cherished possessions.

Somehow he had to deal with the problem he was faced with—the fate he wasn't quite ready to accept.

He needed time.

Chapter 14

Lorren leaned against the kitchen counter and braced herself for the question she knew Mama Nora was about to ask. It would be the same question Rhonda and Rod had asked her at the beginning of the week when she'd stopped by their house to see the baby. It would be the same question Syneda had asked when she'd flown in for a brief visit a few days ago.

"Where's Justin?"

Misery welled up inside Lorren and she brushed away tears that clouded her eyes. She'd sworn she wouldn't cry. But here she was doing just that, partly because she didn't have an answer to the question. The truth of the matter was that she didn't know exactly where Justin was. For the past week, he'd been avoiding her like the plague.

It had started the day after the incident with Scott. That morning, instead of staying and having breakfast with her as he usually did, Justin had told her he needed to go back to his own place to do a few things before leaving for the office. And then, later that day, he'd called to say he had too much paperwork to complete for them to have dinner together.

That day had established a pattern that would be repeated for the rest of the week. She knew he would leave his house before she would awaken in the morning, and would return home from work late at night. He had completely stopped coming over to her place.

At first she had thought his withdrawal had something to do with the incident involving Scott, but now she wasn't certain of anything.

"Lorren? Child, what's the matter?"

Lorren sniffed and brushed her hand across her face again. "I'm sorry, Mama Nora. I didn't invite you to dinner to—"

She couldn't finish what she'd been about to say when she found herself enveloped in the older woman's warm embrace.

"Come on, baby, let's go in the living room and sit a spell. Dinner can wait. I want you to tell Mama what's wrong."

"But that's just it. I don't know what's wrong. All I know is that Justin is putting distance between us and I don't know why. He didn't give me a reason." She then told Mama Nora how Justin had begun avoiding her.

Lorren sniffed again when they reached the living room and, together, they sat on the sofa. "But then an explanation really isn't necessary, is it. He no longer wants me. There were never any promises of forever. I knew that and loved him anyway."

"So you do love him?"

Lorren looked stunned. "Of course I love him. He's the kindest, most tenderhearted, loving man I know. It's not his fault that I read more into our relationship than what was really there," she said through her tears. "I'm just not the woman he needs. I'm not the woman he's been waiting for."

"Have you thought that maybe there's another reason why he's avoiding you?"

Lorren frowned. "What other reason could there be?"

"The boy just might be scared, Lorren. Maybe you are the woman he's been waiting for, and he just can't deal with it."

Confusion showed in Lorren's face. "I don't understand."

Mama Nora hugged Lorren tenderly. "Have you ever heard the old saying—'Be careful what you ask for, you just might get it'?"

Lorren nodded.

"I think Justin has gotten just what he asked for,

and now he can't deal with having it. But you shouldn't give up on him, baby. The boy will come around when he realizes how much he loves you."

He missed Lorren.

Justin had a hard time sleeping—waking often, tumbling about. Even after a week, he still missed the feminine body he'd grown used to sleeping next to.

Tired of tossing and turning, he rose from the bed and pulled on his jeans. In the living room he sat down on the sofa and reached for the small framed photograph Clayton had taken of him and Lorren after the cookout. Gazing at the picture, memories tugged at him.

They were memories of the night he had seen Lorren for the first time at Ms. Nora's party, the shocked look on her face when he'd told her he was her neighbor, and an even more shocked look when he had agreed to go along with her preaffair agreement.

He would never forget the sight of her standing in the doorway when he'd returned to her house the night of the car accident. And he would always have memories of the time they had spent together on the camping trip, the night she had run to him in the storm, and the first time they had made love.

Closing his eyes, he recaptured the look of impassioned surrender on her face whenever his body joined hers, and her expression of utter satisfaction when their bodies climaxed simultaneously.

A deep groan escaped his throat. He reopened his eyes and was filled with wonder at the enormity of all the things they had shared. His fingers gripped the frame until they hurt. Carefully, he relaxed his hand, but not his mind. It was still in turmoil. He replaced the photograph on the table.

Standing, he walked to the window and gazed out at the lake. Moonlight brought a magic aura to the water, and the tops of nearby trees stirred with the whisper of a warming breeze. His hand stroked the windowsill as he stood in deep thought.

He knew he'd hurt Lorren by pulling away without giving her a reason, but what excuse could he have given her?...*I know I love you and that you're my fate but I'm too much of a coward to face it...*

Justin heaved a heavy sigh. He was getting the time he'd felt was needed to work things out within himself. But it didn't keep him from missing her, needing her, loving her. Why was their separation causing him such misery? Such pain?

He walked back into his bedroom. Since sleep was out of the question, he decided to go swimming.

So close together but yet so far apart, Lorren thought, entering the house after returning from taking Mama Nora back home after dinner. Justin's car was parked in front of his place, which meant he was home.

Should she go over and confront him? No. He was the one who had put distance between them without giving her an explanation. If he wanted to talk, he knew where to find her.

She couldn't buy Mama Nora's theory that she was Justin's fate, and he was running scared. It just didn't make sense.

Locking the door behind her, she went into the bedroom to get ready for bed. After taking her shower, she returned to the bedroom and glanced around, wondering where she had put the envelope she planned to mail to her agent. She checked atop the dresser, then pulled open the drawer of the nightstand next to her bed.

"Oh." Lying on top of the envelope she'd been looking for was Justin's medallion.

She fought for control of her muddled emotions. What was Justin's medallion doing in her nightstand drawer? When had he taken it off and placed it there?

Lorren forced herself to remember the last time they had shared her bed. It had been the day Scott had shown up. All that afternoon and night they had made love.

A thrill raced through her as she tried to come to grips with what Justin's removing the medallion could possibly mean. Could Mama Nora be right? Had he actually realized he loved her, and that she had taken Denise's place in his life? Was that what he was fighting?

Lorren replaced the medallion in the drawer. She needed to talk to Syneda. Her friend had always been a good listener. Hurrying to the living room, she placed a phone call to New York.

A sleepy, feminine voice on the other end returned her hello.

"Syneda?"

"Lorren, is that you? What's wrong? Has something happened to Mama Nora?"

Lorren dropped down on the sofa. "No, Mama Nora is fine. She had dinner with me tonight."

There was a pause. "Then what's going on?"

Lorren felt an instant knotting of her stomach. As casually as she could, she asked, "Are you alone?"

Syneda chuckled. "Funny you should ask. I have Mario Van Peebles sleeping right beside me."

Lorren smiled. She knew of her friend's fascination with the handsome model turned actor. "Hmmm, Mario Van Peebles? You don't say?"

"I do say." Syneda giggled. "Shape up, sister-girl, of course I'm alone. What gives?"

Lorren leaned back onto the cushions and picked up a plump pillow. Her fingers traced the patterns of its floral design as she held it close to her. "Justin's still avoiding me."

"Then you need to confront him and find out why."

Lorren caught her lip between her teeth. "Mama Nora has formed her own opinion as to why he's staying away."

She then told Syneda about the conversation she'd had earlier with Mama Nora, and about finding the medallion in the nightstand.

"Ummm, in that case, Mama Nora just might be right, Lorren. Everyone who has ever seen you and Justin together knows how much he adores you, and you of all people know how much that medallion means to him. There has to be a reason why he took it off."

"I hope so."

"If you truly love him, Lorren, you'll fight for him."

"Fight whom? Or what?"

"Whoever or whatever is standing in the way of your having him. You can do it, Lorren, you're a fighter. Go for it."

Lorren drew in a long weary breath as she stood from her seat. She wished she were as convinced of her abilities as her friend. "But what if we're wrong? What if he doesn't really love me?"

"I believe with all my heart that Justin loves you Lorren, and if you'd take a minute to think about it, I know you believe it, too."

"I want to, Syneda."

"Then do it. Justin is nothing like Scott. He's the kind of man dreams are made of. But like all of us, he probably has a few demons to face. Just remember that being in love with someone means helping him through rough times."

"For someone who has never been in love, you sure seem to know a lot about it."

"I read a lot of those romance novels," Syneda teased. "Now can I get back to Super Mario?"

Lorren grinned. "I suppose so."

Syneda laughed. "Gee, thanks. And Lorren, good luck."

A bird chirping outside Lorren's bedroom window awakened her the next morning. Opening her eyes, she knew what had to be done if she wanted to spend the rest of her life with Justin. Deep down she'd known all along.

She would fight for him.

Not because Syneda thought she *should,* but because she believed she *could.* Never before had Lorren possessed so much confidence in herself. She was not the insecure woman who had come to Ennis three months ago. Nor was she the weak woman who'd allowed Scott to brainwash her into believing she was anything less than she was.

She was a woman with guts, strength, and determination. She was a woman who believed in herself, and come hell or high water, Justin would find out that she was not a woman a man could take lightly—or disregard.

He was about to discover that, whether he liked it or not, he had finally met his fate.

"Why do I get the feeling you aren't glad to see us?" Clayton asked his oldest brother as he and Dex sat at the kitchen table watching Justin prepare them breakfast.

"It's all in your mind, Clayton," Justin responded, as he continued scrambling the eggs.

"Is it? Then what's the reason for your funky mood?" Clayton grinned. "It can't be because Dex and I showed up this morning on your doorstep."

Justin eyed his brother crossly. "I'm not in a bad mood," he snapped. "And the two of you don't need an invitation to visit."

Clayton chuckled. "That's good to know. Oh, by the way, where's Lorren?"

Justin sat the plate of eggs in the center of the table. "Home, I'd imagine. Lorren and I aren't seeing each other anymore."

"Why?" Clayton and Dex asked simultaeously.

Justin took his seat at the table. "Why all the interest?"

Dex answered. "I guess we all thought you and Lorren were pretty tight."

"Well, you all thought wrong."

Clayton smiled and rubbed his chin. "So, in that case, you won't have a problem with me, ah, checking her out myself?"

Justin stared at his younger brother. "It won't work, Clayton. I know what you're trying to do, and it won't work."

"What am I trying to do?" Clayton asked innocently.

"You're trying to pull the same stunt on me that you pulled on Dex and Caitlin when they first met. You're going to pretend to be interested in Lorren to make me jealous. Forget it. That stunt may have worked for Dex and Caitlin back then, but it won't work for me."

"Why?" Clayton asked, running the risk of being told it was none of his business. He shrugged. It wouldn't be the first time, and he seriously doubted it would be the last.

"Because Lorren is my fate."

Clayton frowned. "Your fate? That woman you've claimed to have been waiting for all these years?"

Justin nodded.

Clayton shook his head. "Damn, that's scary. All this time I thought you were giving us a bunch of bull about that fate stuff." He took a huge swallow of orange juice.

"Hey, wait a minute," Clayton said moments later. "Then what's the problem if Lorren's your dream girl?"

"The problem is that I don't want to give my heart to anyone completely and totally, ever again. I don't know if I could handle it if I were to ever lose another person. The love I feel for Lorren is a hell of a lot stronger than what I felt for Denise. And you're right, it is scary."

"But think about what you're saying, Justin," Clayton implored. "If Lorren's the woman you've been holding out for all this time, you can't just turn your back on her."

"I'm not turning my back on her, Clayton. I'm just giving myself time to come to terms with it."

"And what's Lorren supposed to be doing while you're taking the time to think things through?"

"Look, Clayton, I really don't expect you to understand any of this. Until you've gone through the pain of loving someone and then losing her, you won't understand."

Clayton Madaris always enjoyed a good argument. And he had no qualms about engaging in one now, especially if it would make Justin see the mistake he was making.

"You aren't thinking straight, Justin. Hell, bro, you're not thinking at all. No man in his right mind breaks up with the woman he loves, especially if it's the woman he's been waiting ten years for." From the expression on Justin's face, Clayton knew Justin had heard his words, but was refusing to let them sink in.

Justin eyed Dex, who had been quiet all this time. "Aren't you going to contribute your two cents, Dex?"

Dex met Justin's glare. "No. We came here to check out this monstrosity of a house you bought, Justin. We aren't here to stick our noses where they don't belong. *Are we,* Clayton Jerome?" he asked his younger brother pointedly.

Clayton smiled. Any other man would have felt outnumbered, but he didn't. He really wasn't surprised by Dex's attitude. He was still hurting from a failed marrlage. lt was bad enough to have one brother suffering from heartache, Clayton thought. He sure didn't want to add Justin to the "pain and suffering" list with Dex, but it appeared that's just where he was headed. Clayton was glad his motto in life was—the only men that aren't fools are bachelors. He was doing the right thing playing the field. This falling in love stuff was far more trouble than it was worth.

"I guess not, Dexter Jordan," Clayton finally replied, grinning at the two brothers he loved and respected. "But I hope the two of you understand that the attorney in me can't resist giving a closing argument. And I promise to make it brief."

Clayton then gave Justin his full attention. "The way I see it, not accepting Lorren as your fate is the same thing as losing her. Either way, she's out of your life forever."

He spooned a hefty serving of eggs onto his plate before continuing. "For ten years you've been tempting fate, and it's time for you to pay up. You're a smart man, Justin, you'll come to your senses and work things out with Lorren when you've had enough. Hopefully, by then, it won't be too late."

Chapter 15

Three days later

Justin had had enough.

Last night had been another sleepless night. He wondered at what point he would stop thinking of Lorren and start sleeping again. When would the memories of the time they'd spent together stop slipping into his thoughts?

Wearily, he slumped back in his desk chair and closed his eyes. Was it possible for someone to escape the world as he knew it and create one of his own—a perfect world? A world free of injustices, disappointments, heartaches, and pain? A world where everything lasted forever?

His eyes flitted open. There was no such thing as a perfect world. The real world was filled with imperfections. Life held no guarantees. You had to take chances.

But if you chose to do so, you could live each day of your life to the fullest, appreciating the time you shared with that special person.

In the real world only the strong survived.

He straightened in his chair. Was he such a weakling that he was willing to let his fear of the unknown destroy him and what he could have with the woman he loved? The woman he'd been waiting for.

Justin inhaled sharply, finally able to confront his fears. Clayton had presented a good argument. Would not accepting Lorren as his fate make the pain easier to bear when he lost her?

No! He needed her like he needed the very air he breathed. He loved her too much to let his fear keep them apart.

Now that you've finally gotten your act together, there's something you need to think about. You love Lorren, but she may not love you. She's never said she did. In fact, she said she stopped believing in love and marriage a long time ago.

He stood quickly. No matter what his mind was saying, Lorren loved him. Over the past months, she'd said it in every way but with words. He'd felt it every time he held her in his arms and when his body joined with hers. No woman gave herself to a man the way she'd given herself to him without love. Lorren was a woman made for love, his love. She was the woman he'd dreamed of finding for ten lonely years.

Picking up a slip of paper from his desk, he quickly scanned it. Lorren had called earlier while he was with a patient. She'd left a message asking him to meet her at Taylor Oaks at four o'clock.

He smiled. He was giving up his fight with fate, accepting defeat graciously. And he would thank God every day for bringing Lorren into his life.

The builders doing the renovations had finished for the day and were leaving when Lorren arrived at Taylor Oaks. The carpenters had already arranged a portion of the downstairs, converting it into Justin's medical office. She'd been thrilled that he had agreed with all of her suggestions and decided not to cover the beautiful oak floors with carpeting.

Lorren paced the floor, nervously waiting for Justin to arrive. "Too late to get cold feet now," she muttered to herself. But she couldn't help the fluttering of her heart when she heard his car pull up.

Justin entered the house, closing the door behind him. He found Lorren in the living room, enclosed by crates and boxes and looking completely out of place in the chaotic surroundings.

She was dressed in a peach-colored suit made of soft silk and matching heels. The outfit was stylishly sculptured to fit the curves of her body. The straight skirt hit her knees, showing long, beautiful legs. He'd known the first time he'd seen her—the night of Ms. Nora's party—that her legs were perfect. That everything about Lorren was perfect. And he'd discovered just how right she was for him in every way.

A fancy peach-colored wide brim cuff hat adorned her head. She wore a diamond necklace and matching diamond stud earrings. She looked stunning, and the sight of her nearly took his breath away.

"You look sensational, Lorren. Where're you going?"

Lorren's pulse quickened upon seeing Justin. "To a wedding." Her nerves tingled. She had to be strong. Their future depended on it. "The reason I asked you to meet me is because there's a couple of things I'd like to say to you, Justin."

He gazed at her. "There's a few things I'd like to say to you, too, Lorren."

"I'll go first, if you don't mind."

"All right." Justin leaned against the wall. He watched Lorren pace the floor a few times before coming to a stop in front of him.

"I'd like to return this," she said, handing him the medallion. "You left it at my house the last time we were together."

She hesitated for a brief moment before continuing. "On the night we met, Justin, you said you believed in fate and that one day fate would bring this special woman to you. At the time, I thought you were living in a dream world, and I was realistic enough to know things just didn't happen that way. And I believe that deep down, you knew that, too. You just didn't want to admit it."

She paused for a moment. "I now realize that you were still hurting that night, just as I was. You just developed a different way of dealing with the pain, which was convincing yourself that one day you could love again, and that you *would* love again. You conveniently left your future in the hands of fate."

Lorren frowned up at him. "The only problem with that, Justin Madaris," she said, tapping the point of her well-manicured finger several times on his chest, "is your refusal to accept your fate when it came knocking on your door. You may have believed in love and marriage as you claimed, but you never had any intentions of involving yourself with either one again."

"Lorren," Justin broke in, taking her hand in his before she tapped a hole in his chest. "Lorren, I—"

"I'm not through saying what I have to say, so please don't interrupt."

She took her hand from his and looked deep into his eyes. "Well, I've got news for you. I love you, Justin, and I intend to spend the rest of my life loving you. I won't let you go. And if there's anything I've learned about myself in the last few months, it's that I go after what I want. And once it's mine, I'm not about to let go."

She poked his chest once more with her finger. "So take a good look, Justin. Take a real good look because, as far as I'm concerned, I'm your fate whether you like it or not."

Lorren sighed deeply. There. She'd said what was on her mind. Now for the really daring part. She pulled an envelope out of her purse.

"This is for you," she said, handing it to him.

Justin's brow lifted as he eyed the envelope she held out to him. His gaze returned to her, confusion revealed clearly in his features. "What is it?"

"Read it and see."

Justin remembered another time they'd shared a similar scenario. He opened the envelope and pulled out an elegantly designed card and read it.

His head shot up. He stared at her. One look at her face was enough to assure him this was not a joke this time.

He was invited to a wedding. Theirs.

Lorren awoke the next morning, cradled in Justin's arms. Last night he had carried her to thrilling heights during their lovemaking. He'd fulfilled her every dream and had lavished her with the most secure feeling of belonging and love she'd ever known. She smiled as she lay contented in his warmth, knowing she was truly and completely loved.

Justin roused himself from blissful slumber and shifted his gaze to Lorren. Her smile widened when their eyes met.

"Good morning, Mrs. Madaris." Raising his hands, he captured a mass of silky brown hair and brought it to his lips.

"Good morning," she replied in a voice barely above a whisper. "Did you sleep well?"

Justin's eyes turned a deep brown as he ran a hand along Lorren's body. "I didn't sleep at all. I've been taking little catnaps. I have this demanding wife who married me for my body."

Lorren leaned upward and placed a kiss on his jaw. "Oh, yeah? And what did you marry her for?"

His expression became serious. Lorren drew a steady breath when she saw the intense look of love in his eyes. "For all the love the two of us will share forever."

"Ummm, that sounds wonderful."

"It *is* wonderful," Justin replied, pulling her atop him. "It's undeniably wonderful."

She took his face in her hands. "I hope you don't feel you were forced into marrying me yesterday. You handled it admirably, though, and didn't seem at all upset to discover I had a wedding service all planned."

"I had no reason to be upset. I was elated." He grinned. "I'm just glad you timed the ceremony to at least let me shower and change first," he said, placing a kiss on her cheek.

She smiled. "Only because Syneda's plane was late."

He chuckled. "I'm a bit curious as to how you pulled it off so quickly?"

Lorren grinned. "Clayton was real eager to help. He said with you happily married off, he'd only have Dex to deal with on the 'pain and suffering' list." She lifted her brow. "I gather that's a 'male thing' and you understand what he means by that?"

At Justin's nod, she continued. "Well, anyway, Clayton basically took care of everything, especially pulling the strings for the quickie marriage license. He has friends in high places who were willing to make a few exceptions here and there."

Justin laughed, thinking those friends of Clayton's were probably all females. "A few exceptions? Honey, it seemed to me like quite a number of exceptions were made. But I don't care as long as everything's legal."

"Trust me. Everything's legal. We're very much married." She gazed at the sparkling diamond ring on her finger and the matching wedding band. Justin had surprised her with both at the ceremony. She'd been knocked off her feet when he'd told her he had stopped by a jewelry store on his way out to Taylor Oaks for their meeting. He had accepted her as his fate and had every intention of asking her to marry him once he got there. His other surprise was changing the name of the ranch from Taylor Oaks to Lorren Oaks. A new marker had been ordered already.

"Thanks to you, Lorren, I don't have any fears

of my tomorrows," he said huskily. "In fact, I'm looking forward to them."

"And thanks to you, Justin, I'm cured of divorcitis."

In a smooth movement he shifted positions and rolled her beneath him. He smiled. "I told you from the beginning all you needed was a dose of tender, loving care."

Lorren's arms locked around his neck. She breathed in the tantalizing male scent of him. "You may have given me too much TLC, Dr. Madaris. I think I'm addicted. I hope you're prepared to feed my habit." She nuzzled her face against his neck. "I may as well warn you, I'm plagued with a new condition."

"Oh?" Justin asked, pulling her closer to him. "And what condition is that?"

Lorren gazed into the eyes of the man she loved. "Happyitis," she replied silkily. "Is there a cure?"

His eyes met hers. Love shone through in them. "No, sweetheart, there's no cure for happyitis," he answered, brushing his mouth across hers. "It's terminal."

Epilogue

A Year Later

"You're doing great. Just continue to breathe deeply, love."

Lorren bit her bottom lip and breathed as her husband instructed. She sighed with relief as the pain ebbed.

Justin wiped his brow. "I never thought the day would come when I'd be delivering my own child."

"You're doing a great job, Doc," Lorren assured him, just before another hard contraction hit her.

"Hold on, baby. It's almost over." Justin's hand pressed her stomach. "Give me one final big push."

Lorren pushed at the same time grinding agony

tore into her. She felt the baby's head slip from her body and into its father's waiting hands. A split second later, the sound of a wailing baby rent the air.

"It's a girl, Lorren! We have a daughter and she's beautiful!"

Justin held their daughter and grinned proudly, tears misting his eyes as he placed their newborn child on Lorren's chest. He gazed down at his wife with a soft look of love on his features. "Now will you tell me the name you've decided on?"

Tears shone in Lorren's eyes as she held in her arms the product of her and Justin's love. "Yes." She smiled up at him. "Because I know our daughter will be her daddy's girl, it seems fitting to name her after you. Her first name will be Justina. And for her middle name," Lorren said softly, "I want to name her after a person I've never met, but one I've grown to admire and respect. She's a person I owe a lot to for having a hand in making you the man you are today. I'll always be grateful to her for giving you a reason to believe in love and marriage, and for you caring enough to make me believe in them again, too. Her middle name will be Denise. Our daughter's name will be Justina Denise Madaris."

Justin wiped the moisture from his eyes, tears of joy and happiness. "Thank you, baby, for proving there's always tomorrow."

He smiled warmly as he lovingly touched his wife's cheek and gazed down at the gift of love she had just given him. He also thought about Vincent, the little boy they had adopted not long after he and Lorren were married, who was now their son. Justin was overwhelmed by the intensity of emotion he felt for his wife, his daughter, and his son.

His gaze moved from his daughter and fastened intently on Lorren. She was his, to love and to cherish. And he would always do both. He knew his forever had begun the night he'd met his fate.

* * * * *